Secret Agent

Secret Agent

by robyn freedman spizman
& mark johnston

Atheneum Books for Young Readers
New York London Toronto Sydney

Atheneum Books for Young Readers
An imprint of Simon & Schuster Children's Publishing Division
1230 Avenue of the Americas
New York, New York 10020

Book design by Kristin Smith
The text of this book is set in Charter ITC and Courier.
Manufactured in the United States of America
First Edition
2 4 6 8 10 9 7 5 3 1
Library of Congress Cataloging-in-Publication Data
Spizman, Robyn Freedman.
Secret agent / Robyn Freedman Spizman and
Mark Johnston.—1st ed.
p.   cm.
Summary: With help from his friends, New York City
high-school student Kyle Parker sets out to save his parents'
marriage by trying to get his father's novel published.
ISBN 0-689-87044-2
[1. Family problems—Fiction. 2. Publishers and publishing—
Fiction. 3. Authorship—Fiction. 4. New York (N.Y.)—Fiction.]
I. Johnston, Mark, 1948– II. Title.
PZ7.S759Se 2005
[Fic]—dc22   2003028154

To my devoted family and friends.
It's no secret how much I love you.
—R. S.

To Susan Cyr and the memory of my mother,
Grace Scheer
—M. J.

And to all the Kyle Parkers of the world,
who never ever give up on a dream.
—R. S. and M. J.

Acknowledgments

My deepest thanks to my husband, Willy, and our children, Justin and Ali, whose endless affection and love keep me going. To my devoted parents, Jack and Phyllis Freedman, who have always said I could do anything I put my mind to. To my brother, Doug Freedman, and his real-life Genie, who have always served as a constant source of support and inspiration; Doug, thank you for believing in *Secret Agent* and for being such an amazing brother. Thanks to my devoted and wonderful brother-in-law, Dr. Sam Spizman, and his wonderful Gena (hooray!). My unending thanks to Betty Storne, our family angel—you are one of life's truest treasures. My deepest thanks to Richard Arlook for his encouragement while writing this book and to Jack Morton for his unwavering friendship and support. My unending appreciation to Lois and Jerry Blonder, Ramona Freedman, and to the rest of my beloved family and dedicated friends (it's no secret who you are!)—you support me at every turn, and I'm one very lucky girl to have you all in my life. —*R. S.*

Thanks to my teachers Janet Burroway and the late Jerry Stern. Thanks to Nancy Dasenbrock and to the late Bill Steeler for supporting me in the beginning. Thanks to Betsy Gattis for being my best audience. Thanks to Lynn Clark for telling me to start writing children's stories again. Thanks to Anna and Jim for making me look so good. Thanks to Andy for never giving up on the old jokes. And, of course, thanks to my family—Aunt Margaret, King, David, Nan, and, especially, Maggie for reading my stuff. —*M. J.*

No book is ever completed without a slew of secret agents working their magic. Our endless thanks to the devoted Ron and Mary Lee Laitsch of Authentic Creations for serving as our secret agents and making a match that gave roots and wings to this project. Thanks to our talented editor, Susan Burke, for her passion, enthusiasm, and encouragement. Also, thanks to Heidi Hellmich and Jeannie Ng for helping us get it right, and to Polly Kanevsky for the very cool jacket design. And, finally, thanks to Krestyna Lypen for liking the story in the first place. —*R. S. and M. J.*

Chapter 1

"The end!"

Funny way to start a story, but these are the two words that Kyle Parker heard his mom shout at his dad through the thick walls of their brownstone on Twentieth Street between Eighth and Ninth Avenues in New York City at four minutes before midnight on Wednesday, June 9, two weeks and one day before Roosevelt High School got out for the summer.

"Did you hear me, Walter? I said I've had it!"

"I heard you. Everybody in Manhattan heard you. Including our son."

"Kyle's asleep."

"I doubt it."

So did Kyle. But maybe he was wrong. Maybe he was dreaming. And maybe his mother wasn't really telling his father she'd had it. And worse, much worse, calling him by his name.

That's right. Kyle's mom told Kyle's dad she'd had it a lot. Mostly with the book Kyle's dad had been writing for the past six years called *Love in Autumn*. Which, if you asked Kyle, was about as sappy as you could get. The name of the book. I mean, who wants to read a book about love? In autumn? Which just happened to be when Kyle's mom and dad first met.

November 14.

On the skating pond.

In Central Park.

Which was autumn. Or fall. Or whatever you want to call it. Like I said, Kyle called it sappy. And figured that was why no one would publish *Love in Autumn* and send his dad some money. Which was the real reason Kyle's mom told Kyle's dad she'd had it. Because she was sick of being the one who earned all the money all the time. Even when Kyle's dad reminded her she didn't earn *all* the money, since Kyle's dad worked at the Open Book in Greenwich Village four nights a week.

"That's a part-time job for a high school kid!" Kyle's mom answered back. "Not for a grown man with a wife and a son and responsibilities!"

And stomped out of the room.

And slammed the door.

But never—not once, not ever—did she call him by his name.

Until tonight.

Chapter 2

Kyle wasn't the best-looking kid at Roosevelt High School. Nor the most popular. Nor the best athlete. But he wasn't a loser, either. I mean, girls liked him. Or, at least, some did. Or, at least, Lucinda Winston did. But she lived across the street. And still went to PS 126. And worse, way worse, had freckles.

Not that Kyle had anything against freckles. But what would his friends say? Which was a pretty stupid question since he knew exactly what they'd say. And, yeah, this is a delicate subject we're talking about here. I mean, Kyle knew there was nothing wrong with freckles, and anyone who thought different was stupid or prejudiced or both. So he just pretended that freckles had nothing to do with it and convinced himself that Lucinda was just too young (a whole six and a half months younger than he was) and lumped her into the kid category. Which, as you might imagine, thrilled Lucinda no end. In other words, it made her so furious there were times she hated the very mention of the name Kyle Parker. Which, of course, was another way of saying she had a mad crush on him.

Did she mind that his knees were bigger than his calves and that his elbows were bigger than his forearms and that his hair stuck up like the crown of a rooster?

Nope.

Kyle was smart like his dad and hardworking like his mom and knew computers better than anyone on the planet. At least, that was the way Lucinda saw it. Though it wasn't what made her eyelashes curl and her big toes tingle anytime Kyle even glanced in her direction. It was his smile. His special smile. Which, Lucinda realized, was as corny as all get-out. Especially since he saved it for his dog.

Shakespeare.

That's right. That was the dog's name. Which was a pretty high-class name for a dog, any dog, especially a dog as goofy as this dog. Plus, he wasn't even Kyle's dog. You see, Kyle's dad was allergic. So, as far as Kyle's house was concerned, there may as well have been a sign above the door that read No Dogs Allowed (or cats or canaries, for that matter). Another kid may have turned sulky. But that wasn't Kyle's style. He became a professional dog walker. That's right. He walked Shakespeare for money. Because some dog owners, no matter how much they loved their dogs, either didn't have the time or didn't make the time to watch their four-legged friends take a dump.

Sound gross?

Not to Kyle.

He was crazy about Shakespeare—pooper-scooper and all—even before four o'clock that afternoon. When Shakespeare changed everything forever.

But we're getting ahead of ourselves.

Because it wasn't 4 P.M. It was 7 A.M. The morning after the night Kyle heard his mom shout, "The end!" Which meant Kyle wasn't thinking about Shakespeare. Or even his mom sitting across the breakfast table, biting her lower lip. He was thinking about his stomach. Which felt as if someone had tied it into a knot and yanked it so tight he was afraid he might double over and smash, face first, into his Grape-Nuts flakes. Kyle heard a grumbling noise. It sounded like a locomotive. Only it wasn't roaring down the tracks. It was inside his head. Getting louder. And louder. Until Kyle knew there was only one question that could stop it. Not by slamming on the brakes. But by turning his life into a head-on collision.

"Where's Dad?" Kyle said.

Chapter 3

This isn't easy to say about a mother, any mother, especially Kyle's mother, since Kyle wasn't doing all that hot at the moment. But Polly Parker was cut-and-dry. What I mean is, there was no middle ground with Kyle's mom. Things were either good or bad. Right or wrong. No compromises. No second-guessing. Once she made up her mind, that was it. Finished. End of story. You might consider this hard-hearted. But as far as Mrs. Parker was concerned, she'd been raising two kids the past six years. And one of them happened to be her husband.

"Kyle, your father won't be living here any longer," she said.

She didn't shrug. She didn't reach across the table and hold Kyle's hand. She didn't say, "I'm sorry." Because that was another thing about Kyle's mom. She got right to the point. No shilly-shallying or dillydallying. Life was what it was. And it didn't get any better if you tried to dress it up with whipped cream and a cherry on top.

"Why?" Kyle said.

"I think you know why," his mom said.

So okay. So it's time we said something nice about Mrs. Parker. Which, actually, isn't all that difficult. Because Mrs. Parker probably worked as hard at her profession as anyone you will ever meet. Plus, she was great at it.

Great as a what?

As a headhunter.

No, she didn't shrink human skulls and stick them on the ends of spears. A headhunter is business lingo for someone who gets people jobs. Lawyer jobs. Teacher jobs. Executive assistant jobs. All kinds of jobs. And, yeah, Mrs. Parker got paid. And, yeah, she and her family needed the money. But money wasn't the only reason she was so dedicated.

You see, Mrs. Parker believed that the right person in the right job for the right amount of money gave that person self-respect. Which was why she worked ten hours a day five days a week. I don't mean she showed up. I don't mean she put in her time. I mean, once she took you on as a client, it was pretty much a done deal that you were no more than three weeks away from starting your career.

And that wasn't all. She had another great quality. Mrs. Parker loved Kyle the way Kyle loved Shakespeare.

Totally.

Unconditionally.

The no-compromising part of her personality?

That had nothing to do with Kyle. Oh, sure, he had to drink his milk and do his homework and be polite and get to bed on time. There was no cutting corners on any of that stuff. But with the big stuff, the stuff that mattered, the stuff that gave Kyle confidence and made him feel secure, Mrs. Parker never wavered.

Not once.

Not ever.

So don't worry. Kyle wasn't shaking in his socks that if he chewed with his mouth open he'd be out the door with his dad. As far as Kyle's mom was concerned, there was the rest of the world, and then there was Kyle, and Mrs. Parker was as fierce as a grizzly bear when it came to protecting her cub.

Which was what she figured she was doing now. Protecting Kyle by giving it to him straight. No false hope. No pretending things might get better. Kyle's father was gone. She kicked him out. Deal with it.

"For good?" Kyle said.

"Yes, Kyle."

"No chance you'll get back together?"

"No chance."

"None?"

Mrs. Parker didn't answer. Not out loud. Instead, she closed her eyes. And took a deep breath. And, in spite of herself, she reached across the table and took hold of her son's hand. Because, remember, this was Kyle. The crack in her armor. And she was hurting him. And she knew it. And she'd rather rip her arm off at the socket than hear that tone in his voice or see that look in his eyes.

"What can I do, Kyle?" she finally said. "It's the book. He's been writing it for six years. Six years, Kyle. Without a penny. I have dreams too. I'm working ten hours a day, and for what? I want you to go to a good college. I want you to have everything you deserve. You're a smart boy, Kyle, and I can't keep paying the bills on your father's dream. It's killing me. I can't stand it any longer."

And she broke down. Right there at the kitchen table. Which may not sound odd to you. But as far as Kyle was concerned it was like the moon exploding or Tiger Woods hitting a drive less than two hundred yards. Kyle tried to move but couldn't. He tried to speak but couldn't do that, either.

So he just sat there.

Stunned.

Not just because of his mom's tears. But also because of her last sentence. "I can't stand *it* any longer," she'd said. Not *him*. She hadn't said, "I can't stand *him* any longer." She'd said *it*. Which meant his dad wasn't killing her. The book was. Because it wasn't earning any money. Because it wasn't published. Which meant Kyle had to do something. He had to figure out a way to make sure *Love in Autumn* got published. No matter what. No matter where. Then maybe, just maybe, his mom and dad might get back together.

But how do you get a book published?

Huh?

How?

Chapter 4

A few years ago Twentieth Street would have been a maze of broken glass and Coke cans and half-eaten doughnuts for Kyle to hop over or zigzag around or crack or pop or squish. But no more. It was still a city block. Garbage cans still stood guard by the curbs. But the city sweepers had begun to keep the streets clean. And the folks who lived in the neighborhood stopped being litterbugs. And I'm not trying to compare New York to Oz, where Dorothy could have followed the Yellow Brick Road barefoot. I'm just saying Kyle no longer had to scrape his shoes every fifteen steps or hold his nose when he passed the alley behind the pizza parlor on his way to school.

One thing hadn't changed, however. Lucinda still passed him three days a week. Not five days. That would have been too obvious. And not the same days. That would have also been too obvious. Because that's what you did when you had a mad crush on someone who didn't have a mad crush back. You studied his schedule. You found out where he was going to be and when he was going to be there. And then you showed up.

And ignored him.

Totally.

Which was what Lucinda was doing at that very moment. She was pushing open her front door and skipping down the steps. Her sandy blond hair bouncing. Her clogs clicking the concrete. Her T-shirt showing off just enough of her belly to make her dad spill his coffee all over the morning newspaper.

Did Kyle check her out?

Nope.

Lucinda knew. She peeked. Through the same wraparound sunglasses that Carrie-Anne Moss wore in *The Matrix*. She wore the sunglasses so Kyle couldn't see her eyes. Since she wasn't really ignoring him, but only pretending. Which only worked if the guy wasn't ignoring you. Which he was. As far as Kyle was concerned, Lucinda may as well have been a crack in the sidewalk. Better if she had been. At least he was stepping on that. Which was when it hit Lucinda, like a sock on the jaw. Kyle wasn't ignoring her. He didn't even know she existed.

Can you blame him?

Don't get me wrong. It's not that Kyle had never been faced with a problem before. Like two months ago when he wanted to wear his Dave Matthews T-shirt to a Mets game and it was still in the wash. Or last Tuesday when he had to choose between cheesecake and a chocolate sundae for dessert because his mom told him he couldn't have both. But neither of these was in quite the same category as getting your dad's book published to save your parents' marriage. Especially if it was a book you hadn't even read. Not a chapter. Not a page. Not even the first sentence.

Why?

Simple. His dad wouldn't let anyone near it. Including Kyle's mom. Oh, sure, he sent it to editors at publishing houses. And they read it. Or didn't read it. And sent it back rejected. And then Kyle's dad rewrote it. And sent it out again. And it got rejected again. And, of course, Kyle's dad kept a copy for himself. But only one. And a backup disk.

He locked the copy in his top desk drawer. He locked the disk inside his wall safe behind a beat-up framed photograph that he'd had bought at the flea market on Twenty-sixth Street. And not just any photograph. But a photograph of Ernest Hemingway. Who, Kyle's dad told Kyle about six million times, was his hero. Because he wrote *The Old Man and the Sea*. Which was Kyle's dad's all-time favorite. Which didn't surprise Kyle. The old man part, I mean. Since the guy in the photograph had a thick, white, old-man beard and tired, angry, old-man eyes.

It was the eyes that always got to Kyle. They never blinked. They never moved. They just stared at you in kind of a dare. As if they were saying, "Let's see what you got." Like life was a race. And if you weren't trying to win, then what the heck were you doing on the track?

But there was something else. Not in the photograph. But the way it was framed. Or, more precisely, on the brown paper that sealed the back so no dust could get inside the frame. Glued to the paper was a pocket. You know, to hold something. Hold what, no one knew for sure. Since the pocket was empty. Long empty, probably. Though that hadn't stopped Kyle's dad from making up a story right there on the spot.

"Can you feel it, Kyle?" he'd said. And flicked his eyebrows. And winked. "This is no ordinary photograph. Not even close. It was a gift from Ernest Hemingway to one of his children. That's why that pocket is here. To hold his note: 'From Papa. With all my love.'"

"Oh, please!" Kyle's mom had said.

"Close your eyes, Polly. Run your fingers over the glass. The great man touched this. He gripped it in his hands."

"I'd like to grip you in my hands."

"Where's your imagination, Polly? Where's your sense of adventure? This photograph's an omen. It's going to bring us luck."

"It's a waste of money."

"No, Polly. Trust me on this one. I'm buying it. I'm hanging it over the wall safe in the office. And someday

you'll thank me. Someday you'll say it's the best invest-
ment we ever made. You know why, Kyle?"

"Because you can find anything anywhere," Kyle
had said.

"That's right, son. You can find anything anywhere."

Which was a quote from *Cadillac Jack,* a book by
Larry McMurtry. You see, Kyle's dad always quoted
books. Especially that book. Especially that quote. "You
can find anything anywhere." It was kind of like Kyle's
dad's code. The words he lived by. Though none of
it meant all that much to Kyle. Since he'd never read
Cadillac Jack. Or *The Old Man and the Sea.* Or, for that
matter, was he dying to read either one.

Love in Autumn?

That was different.

Why?

Because it was his dad's book. His dad's dream.
Which had now become Kyle's dream. So, yeah, Kyle was
going to read it. Not because he figured anything his dad
wrote would be chock-full of androids or gladiators or
someone sucking blood from someone else's neck. But if
your major goal in life was to come up with a way to get
your dad's book published, it probably helped if you
knew something about that book. Which in Kyle's case
meant he had to read it. Which meant he had to steal it.
Which tightened that knot in his stomach. Which was
pretty darned tight to begin with.

So I guess we can forgive Kyle for not knowing Lucinda existed. Since he didn't know anyone existed. Not the guy on the corner without any shoes, mumbling, "Spare a quarter?" Not the taxi driver running the red light and nearly sideswiping the umbrella stand. Not even Ruben Gomez calling him (Kyle) "Chicken Legs" four hours later during gym.

Because Kyle was in a zone.

A zone all his own.

And he pretty much stayed that way. Until the school bell rang after last period. And Kyle burst out of geometry and ran every step of the way to Greenwich Avenue. Even after his lungs turned to fire. Even after his backpack felt like it weighed a ton. Because Kyle knew exactly where his dad was. And even more important—at least, to Kyle—he knew his dad would be waiting.

Chapter 5

Buzz!

That was the sound of the doorbell to the smallest bookstore in New York City. And not just the smallest. But the one with the most dust. The way Kyle saw it, anyone who could stay inside the Open Book for more than ten minutes and not sneeze deserved an Olympic gold medal.

Why the doorbell?

To make sure no one snuck in and stole a book. Which Kyle never quite understood. I mean, who would want to steal a book? And, even if someone did, who would want to steal an old book? Because they were. Old, I mean. Really old. Printed before Kyle was born. Plus, they were stacked so high and crammed so close that anyone grabbing a hundred-year-old copy of *Pride and Prejudice* or *David Copperfield* and trying to make a run for it would more than likely cough to death before he made it out of that bookshelf maze.

Mr. Jacobson owned the Open Book. Which meant he was Kyle's dad's boss. If boss was a good word. Since

Mr. Jacobson treated Kyle's dad more like a son than an employee. Mr. Jacobson was about seventy years old and walked with a cane and smelled like his books and looked like the rat in the *Charlotte's Web* illustrations. Which was pretty much the exact opposite of his personality. Since Kyle had never met anyone with a kinder voice. Or a more generous heart. Especially if you were Kyle's dad. And not a book thief.

"Hello, Mr. Jacobson."

"Hello, Kyle."

"How's my dad?"

"How do you think?"

I know. That conversation doesn't exactly take Mr. Jacobson out of the rat category. But words don't always tell the whole story. You see, Mr. Jacobson also shrugged. And shook his head. As if to say, "I'm sorry. I wish I could help. I wish I could do something."

As if he already hadn't.

Because there was something else about the Open Book I haven't mentioned yet. Smack dab in the middle of all that dust and clutter was a wraparound, metal staircase. Like a corkscrew. Spiraling straight up. Past the Hawthornes and Twains and Dickenses and Tolstoys until it dead-ended on a landing two feet under this wooden trapdoor that pushed open right onto the second floor. Which, Kyle knew without asking, was where his dad was staying.

How?

Because the rent was free. Because that was the kind of a guy Mr. Jacobson was.

"I'm going up," Kyle said.

"You know the way," Mr. Jacobson said.

And Kyle did. Three summers before, he'd spent half of July pretending the winding stairs were part of a pirate ship and the trapdoor led to a secret compartment where he hid his gold doubloons. Only this time, as he clanked up toward the ceiling, a tingle shot up his spine. Not because he was scared. But because it was just too weird that his old playhouse was now his dad's apartment. Though *apartment* was kind of stretching it, since the whole thing consisted of one room, with a hot plate for a kitchen and a bathroom the size of a phone booth.

There was no tub.

No shower.

No place to clean yourself besides the sink. One sink. Where you washed your dishes *and* your hands but had to be an acrobat to wash anything else. Which, as it happened, was exactly what Kyle's dad was up to when he heard the knock on the trapdoor. He was splashing water under his arms and sloshing most of it all over the floor. Which wasn't exactly the image he wanted his son to see that day. Since Mr. Parker knew it was Kyle. Since it was ten minutes after school got out. And since Kyle's dad knew that Kyle would have run all the way.

"Be right there!" Kyle's dad tried to shout.

But couldn't. Because he was too nervous. So nervous he forgot to dry his armpits before he buttoned up his Hawaiian shirt. Which made it look like he had two big sweat stains about to flood the palm trees. Which didn't surprise him. Since everything else about that day had been a disaster, so why not *look* like an idiot too? Still, he didn't change. There wasn't any time. He just swallowed. Or tried to swallow. And stumbled over to the door. And took a deep breath. And grabbed hold of the rope. And yanked the trapdoor open.

"Son," he said.

Kyle said nothing. He ran up the last two steps and hugged his father.

So much for sweat stains and wet floors and jumpy nerves. None of it mattered. Not now. Not with his son's arms wrapped around him.

"It's okay, Kyle," he said.

"No, it's not," Kyle said.

"You're right," Kyle's dad said. "I won't lie to you. It's not okay. But it will be. Someday. I promise."

Kyle let go. He let go of his dad, that is. But in the same motion he crossed his arms in front of his chest as if he were hugging himself.

"How?" he said. "How is it going to be okay?"

Silence.

Nothing.

Kyle's dad didn't even shrug.

Which was weird. Way weird. Because Kyle couldn't remember a time his dad didn't have some kind of comeback. Something snappy. Something positive. Because his dad was always positive. Even at his first job. Where he worked ten years as a social worker in an assisted living facility. Which is a polite way of saying an old-folks home. Or, in Mr. Parker's case, an old-folks home where all the people were sick and ready to die.

Tough job?

You bet.

But it was especially tough in the Bronx. Where every day he went to work Mr. Parker saw someone buy drugs or get mugged or run away from the police. He was never robbed himself. Nothing like that. Which was surprising. He wasn't very tall and about as skinny as they come, and if anyone would have stuck a gun or knife in his face he would have given away his money without a fight since he practically gave away all the money he carried in his pockets anyway to anyone who asked.

You see, Kyle's dad was a dreamer. He dreamed that one day people would be nicer to one another and more generous with one another and that no kid would be poor and no old person would be lonely. But that wasn't all he dreamed. He had a different dream, his own dream, a dream he tucked way, way back in the corner of his heart. Don't get me wrong. He wasn't unrealistic. He knew it would take hard work. And maybe even a lot of luck. But Mr. Parker believed that everyone should do something that no one else could do. Something wonderful. Something special. Which was why he finally said good-bye to the old-folks home and started writing his book. Because now he was part of his own dream. No matter how many times Kyle's mom got upset. No matter how many rejection letters came in the mail. Kyle's dad simply smiled, cocked those thin eyebrows of his, and said:

"Just you wait, Henry Higgins!"

Which is what Eliza Doolittle says in *My Fair Lady*. Which was Kyle's dad's favorite musical. And, yeah, it took Kyle a while to realize his dad meant that one day he'd prove all those rejection letters wrong the same way Eliza proves Henry Higgins wrong. But one thing Kyle knew the instant he saw those eyebrows cock. He knew his dad wasn't giving up. That he'd never give up. That he loved his book. He loved writing his book. And the only reason I'm telling you all this stuff is to show how different Kyle's dad was. At that moment. Standing in that apartment. Without his son's arms wrapped around him. Facing the toughest question of his life.

"I'm sorry, Dad!" Kyle said. "I should never have asked you that! You'll figure out how to make it okay! You always have!"

"Sure," Kyle's dad said. "I always have."

But then he sighed.

And his shoulders slumped.

And a chill shot up Kyle's backbone. But not just a chill. There was something else. Something surprising. At least, to Kyle. Because he didn't panic. His knees didn't buckle. He just stood there. Calm. Thinking of baseball.

I swear.

You see, every time they practiced and Kyle would swing and miss, his dad would always throw him another pitch. Well, that's what this was. I mean, Kyle's dad might have struck out. But all he needed to get back in the game was a nice, juicy fast one right down the center of the plate. And, no, Kyle couldn't have told you where that pitch was coming from.

But we could.

If we checked our watches.

Because it was almost four o'clock.

Chapter 6

Greenwich Avenue is weird for Manhattan. Almost every other street on the island is cut on a grid. You know, at right angles. But not Greenwich. It's diagonal. Kind of like the side opposite the right angle in a triangle. Which meant if Kyle stuck to it, he could save walking time. Or so he figured. What he didn't figure was that everybody else heading in his direction figured the same thing. In other words, Greenwich Avenue was mobbed. Which meant Kyle saved steps. But not all that much time. Because he kept slowing down to zigzag around women pushing baby carriages or tourists checking subway maps or dogs on leashes sniffing fire hydrants.

The dogs reminded Kyle of Shakespeare. Which reminded Kyle it was five minutes to four. Which reminded Kyle if he was late he might have to deal with Shakespeare's owner, Percy Percerville. That's right. You heard me. And, yeah, his name was odd. But that was nothing compared to Percy himself, who could have been crowned King Kong of the oddballs.

No one outside his tailor knew what color Percy's

pajamas were. But everyone within a radius of five city blocks knew Percy's shirts, pants, socks, suits, and ties were red. All red. Only red. Which set off his black suede shoes and black bowler hat and black cape rather dramatically. He carried a stick, a walking stick, a twenty-four-carat-gold-tipped walking stick. Which he used to tap strangers on the shoulder before saying such things as: "I'm sorry, dear boy, but no one combs his hair like that on a Tuesday."

Percy had a job. Or, at least, he kept busy. Since he disappeared for weeks at a time. Not abroad or out of the state. He disappeared inside his three-bedroomed, marble-floored, crystal-chandeliered, four-storied town house. And all anyone saw of him was the occasional shadow. Late at night. On the top floor. Behind his off-white, silk curtains. Pacing.

Back and forth.

Back and forth.

Back and forth.

Was he a mad scientist? An FBI agent? A forger of van Goghs and Picassos? There were rumors, to be sure. But there was one thing about Percy Percerville on which everyone in the neighborhood agreed. Percy was the normal one. Boring even. *If* you compared him to Shakespeare.

High-strung, a nipper of ankles, ready to growl and whimper at the same time, Shakespeare was a cross between a Border collie and a dingo, with a dash of Dalmatian thrown in. He was bred to herd sheep. And, since there were no sheep around Twentieth Street, he did his best to herd you. Mothers with young children scooted across the street. Grown men gulped. Dogs rolled over and pretended they were already dead. Picture a small wolf with a patch on his eye who could leap like a dolphin from a standstill, and you get a pretty good idea why taking Shakespeare for a walk was either a ride on a magic carpet or a crawl through quicksand. Depending on the moon. Or the stars. Or some equally mysterious force known only to Shakespeare.

None of which mattered to Kyle. Who adored him. Would have jumped in front of a bus for him. And no telling why. Since the dog was nuts. I mean, one day Kyle would open the door and Shakespeare would get so excited he'd wet the floor. And the next day when Kyle arrived, Shakespeare's ears would drop and his rear end would shake and he'd scamper backward out of the room.

Which was exactly what happened that afternoon.

Of all afternoons.

At twenty-two seconds before four.

The instant he heard Kyle's key in the lock.

Shakespeare let loose with a yelp then scooted out of the room so fast he looked like a whirlpool turned on its side. Maybe because Kyle was so upset about his mom and dad that he gave off a different vibe. Or scent. Whatever. Shakespeare spooked. And split. And left Kyle with no pee to wipe up. But no Shakespeare, either. Which, normally, wouldn't have thrown Kyle into too much of a loop. But that afternoon wasn't normally. And Kyle was. Thrown into a loop, that is.

"Here, Shakespeare! Come on, boy!"

Nothing.

"Shakespeare! Where are you? Time for your walk!"

Still nothing.

And so Kyle waited. Thirty seconds. A minute. A minute and a half. Two minutes and thirty-five seconds. And when he still heard nothing—not a bark or a pant or even paws scratching the marble floor—Kyle snapped. I don't mean he hopped up and down or kicked his feet in the air or started smashing the Inuit sculptures in the cubbyholes of the hallway bookcase.

Instead, he did something worse.

Much worse.

Because there are some things you do that only someone you love can make you do. And sometimes it's great. Like winning the fifty-yard breaststroke for your dad. Or making an A on the chemistry test for your mom. But sometimes it's the exact opposite. Sometimes it's so bad you can't believe you're doing it, even while you're doing it. Which was what happened here. Because, like I said, Kyle snapped. Shakespeare made

Kyle snap. And maybe if Kyle hadn't loved Shakespeare so much, Kyle wouldn't have snapped so hard that he broke the one and only rule Percy Percerville had made Kyle promise he'd never ever break.

He went searching for Shakespeare.

And climbed the stairs.

Chapter 7

Here's what's crazy:

Before the soles of his Nike Cross Trainers touched the first step of Percy Percerville's marble staircase, Kyle Parker had never broken a rule. He'd never crossed the street against the Don't Walk sign. He'd never snuck an extra piece of bubble gum. He'd never talked in class unless he raised his hand. He'd never cut in line. He'd never smoked cigarettes. He'd never spit.

And, yeah, he was planning on swiping a copy of *Love in Autumn*. But planning it and doing it are two different things. And just look at how much of a daze he'd been in since the idea first hit him. Because, basically, Kyle was a good kid. Or, at least, he *tried* to be a good kid. Perfect even. Mostly because his mom and dad always seemed so unhappy with one another that Kyle wanted to make sure they never had a reason to be unhappy with him. But it wasn't easy being perfect. Too much pressure. For too long a time. Until something had to give. Which it did. Right then.

Big-time.

You see, Percy had a rule. One rule. Which he announced to anyone and everyone who entered his house:

"Never climb the stairs."

He didn't explain the rule. He didn't apologize for the rule. That was it. No discussion. End of story. And it worked. Or had. For seventeen years. No one but Percy or Shakespeare had been above the ground floor of Percy Percerville's town house since before Kyle was born. Not Mrs. Bentley, who cleaned on Tuesdays and Saturdays. Or Fred, who delivered meat and fish on Mondays and Thursdays. Or the plumber. Or the painters. Or the mailman. Or even a friend.

If Percy Percerville had any friends.

The neighbors didn't take a poll or anything. But everyone up and down Twentieth Street pretty much agreed that if there was an exception to this rule it was probably Kyle. He had a key to the front door. He could come and go as he pleased. So, even if he'd never been invited upstairs, Kyle could have waited until he was sure Percy wasn't around and, you know, peeked.

But Kyle never peeked. He never even thought about peeking. In fact, Kyle didn't know anything more about Percy Percerville's town house than the baker at the Chelsea Bakery, or the shoe shine girl at Sam's, or anyone else who'd never set foot inside 324 West Twentieth Street. Except that the entrance hall walls were covered with bookshelves filled with sculptures of whales and bears and caribou and musk oxen and lots and lots and lots and lots of books. Because that was all Kyle could see from the chair two feet to the right of the mahogany front door. Which was as far into Percy's town house as Kyle had ever been. Which was the deal. Struck with a handshake on Kyle's first day of employment:

"You shall remain in the entrance hall. Only in the entrance hall. Never any farther than the entrance hall. Am I making myself clear, dear boy? No matter if the house is on fire. No matter if blood drips from the ceiling. You stay here. In this chair. And wait for Shakespeare's return. For he shall return. And I shall pay you to read. Or play with your Palm Pilot. Or do whatever boys your age do when they sit in chairs and wait for dogs."

And that was it. The last they spoke. From that moment on, Percy communicated only through notes.

As in:

Shakespeare seems wistful when I bring up the stock market. Best keep him clear of the Museum of Modern Art for a while. We wouldn't want him to start wearing berets.

Or:

Shakespeare fell asleep with his legs crossed last night. Bravo, dear boy! The yoga lessons are paying off in spades!

These were jokes, of course. Kyle figured that out. But they were something else, too. Something serious. Not the words. The words were silly. But the idea that Percy wrote notes instead of talking to Kyle reinforced the idea that Percy was private. Which, of course, reinforced the rule. The Never-Climb-the-Stairs rule. Which made it even more spectacular when Kyle broke it. Though Kyle wasn't thinking about breaking anything when his foot hit that bottom step. And he heard the creak. And felt the blood vessels in his head constrict. Or expand. Or do whatever blood vessels do when they remind you they are there. Throbbing. As Kyle raced halfway up the stairs.

And froze.

At the sound of Percy Percerville's voice. Which was exploding from the open door of his office. Which Kyle couldn't see. Or even know was an office. Because Kyle wasn't far enough up the stairs to see anything but the final seven steps. Certainly not the second floor. The forbidden floor. Or even know why it was forbidden. But Kyle knew this much. He knew his heart was doing laps around his rib cage. He knew his stomach was trying to turn itself inside out. Because, yeah, Kyle couldn't see Percy. But somehow, some way, Kyle figured Percy must be able to see him.

In other words, Kyle thought he was caught. For one hideous, horrible moment, Kyle thought Percy must be hovering above him or about to pop up like a jack-in-the-box from the top of the stairway.

But, no.

Like I said, Percy was screaming, all right. But he was screaming at Frank Cutter, senior editor at Barcourt Publishers. Not in person. Percy was screaming into a speakerphone on top of his desk:

"No, dear boy, you may not speak with Cynthia Marlow at this or at any other time! You may speak to me! Do I make myself clear, dear boy? Me! Only me! Percy Percerville! Her literary agent. A relationship about which you are sworn—I repeat—*sworn* to secrecy. For if word leaks out I *am* her literary agent or if I ever catch anyone—*anyone*—connected to Barcourt Publishers either following me or in any other way clandestinely trying to discover the exact identity of Cynthia Marlow, all legal agreements signed heretofore *with* Barcourt Publishers *by* Ms. Marlow shall be considered null and void with a vengeance!"

Did Kyle faint?

Run away?

Nope.

He just stood there. Not blinking. Or breathing. Or doing much of anything. Except trying to picture that name.

Cynthia Marlow.

He knew it. He was certain he knew it. He just couldn't remember where he'd seen it. Or heard it. Not while he was scared senseless halfway up Percy Percerville's marble stairs. Until it hit him. The word *literary*. It was like *literature.* Which was like books. Which was when Kyle remembered that he'd seen the name Cynthia Marlow all over the magazine covers in the supermarket checkout line: WHO IS CYNTHIA MARLOW? WHERE IS CYNTHIA MARLOW? CYNTHIA MARLOW—BEST-SELLING AUTHOR OF ALL TIME—NEVER SEEN IN PUBLIC! Which he stopped remembering. At least, for the moment. Because Percy Percerville had started screaming again:

"This is exactly why she hired me, dear boy. To ensure she'll never be subjected to the horror of a television or radio or magazine or newspaper or any other type of interview! So put it out of your mind! For it will never happen, dear boy! And consider yourself blessed that after two blockbuster books a year, every year, for the past seventeen years running, she isn't demanding a bigger percentage of the royalties and that, out of the goodness of her golden heart, she keeps cutting you in on the profits from her movies!"

"Errrrrrr!"

This wasn't Percy. Percy didn't whimper like a dog. Nor did he tuck his tail between his legs as he crept down the stairs. Percy didn't have a tail. And he wasn't the kind to creep. But Shakespeare was. And did. Kyle put his finger to his lips and practically swallowed his tongue as he watched Shakespeare shiver and shake his way down each stair, one nervous paw at a time.

"Shhh!" said Kyle.

"Errrrrr!" repeated Shakespeare.

There was something in Shakespeare's mouth. Which wasn't surprising. When Shakespeare was nervous (and Shakespeare was always nervous), that was the way he greeted you. With something in his mouth. This time it was a sheet of paper. Which he dropped at Kyle's feet. So close Kyle didn't have to pick it up to see it was a title page. To a manuscript. Of a book. Not his dad's book. Not *Love in Autumn*. But a different title page. To a different book:

The Mists of Amore
by
Cynthia Marlow

That's right. The same Cynthia Marlow that Percy had been screaming about over the telephone. Plus, this title page—the one at Kyle's feet—wasn't printed by a computer. It was written by hand. And not just any hand. But the same hand that had written Shakespeare's silly stock market and yoga lesson notes. You know, the notes that had been left on the chair. In Percy Percerville's entrance hall. Two feet to the right of the mahogany front door.

Chapter 8

Kyle got out of there.

Pronto.

He left the title page where it lay, hooked Shakespeare to his leash, and beat it out the door as if there *was* blood dripping from Percy Percerville's ceiling. But while Shakespeare pooped and Kyle scooped then fast walked around the seminary then sat down on the see-saw in the concrete park on Twenty-first Street then scratched Shakespeare's rump then let Shakespeare lick his cheek and nuzzle his nose, Kyle kept asking himself the same question over and over and over again.

Was it fate?

Nah.

Kyle didn't believe in fate. Or, at least, Kyle's dad didn't believe in fate. He told Kyle it was like destiny. No one had any true destiny. You had choices. Free will. If a train hit you, Kyle's dad always said, it had nothing to do with your fate or your destiny. It was because you were too stupid to get off the tracks.

Yeah?

Then how did you explain what had just happened?

Huh?

How did you explain that?

I mean, here Kyle was. Some kid. Whose one and only goal in life was to get his dad's book published so his dad could get some money so his dad could move back home. And what happened? That very same day that very same kid discovered he works for the most successful writer who ever lived. Cynthia Marlow. Except Cynthia Marlow wasn't really Cynthia Marlow. Because Cynthia Marlow didn't exist. Because Cynthia Marlow was really Percy Percerville pretending he wasn't Cynthia Marlow.

Wait a minute!

Wait a minute!

It was coming back to Kyle now. That conversation. The one he had with his dad so long ago—maybe six months—he could barely remember. Kyle had been bored. He remembered that much. Because he and his dad had to go shopping, and the grocery store was crowded, and they were stuck in the checkout line. That was when his dad pointed to the magazine headline. No, not WHO IS CYNTHIA MARLOW? or WHERE IS CYNTHIA MARLOW? or CYNTHIA MARLOW—BEST-SELLING AUTHOR OF ALL TIME—NEVER SEEN IN PUBLIC! Kyle's dad pointed to the other one. The bigger one. The one that took up half the front page:

$10,000 REWARD FOR INFORMATION LEADING
TO THE TRUE IDENTITY OF CYNTHIA MARLOW!

Was it a dream?

Did Kyle dream this?

Nope. That was it. That was the headline. Kyle remembered it now as clearly as he remembered his dad shaking his head and saying, "Why don't they just read her books and leave the poor woman alone?"

Oops!

Too much. Kyle didn't want to remember that part. Or the tone in his dad's voice. Or the way his dad shook his head. Or sighed. Or shook his head all over again. Who needed to remember that stuff? Especially since everything would have been so much easier if Kyle just forgot all about it. I mean, think what was happening here. Kyle needed money. Or, at least, his dad needed money. So if Kyle came up with ten thousand dollars and gave it to his dad, that would answer the problem, right? That would make everything okay, right?

Wrong!

At least, that was what Kyle's gut was telling him. And, yeah, we're talking about ten thousand dollars, so you can bet Kyle was trying hard not to listen. But every time his head said, "You bet! Why not?" his belly turned tight as a fist.

Because he kept seeing the look on his dad's face.

And hearing him sigh.

And not only that. Because even if Kyle had never seen the look of disgust on his dad's face or heard the disapproval in his voice, Kyle would have known deep down in his heart that you didn't turn someone in who didn't want to be turned in if that someone hadn't done anything wrong. Not for ten thousand dollars. Not to get your mom and dad back together. Especially not to get your mom and dad back together. Because it would be a cheat. You'd be a cheat. And your dad still wouldn't be published.

So there he was. Kyle, I mean. Back to fate and destiny. Which wasn't ten thousand dollars. But it was something. And Kyle couldn't help but think it was something important. Maybe the beginning. An idea. Or at least an inkling. That all this was bigger than he was. That he couldn't go it alone. That if he wanted to get his dad's book published he needed help.

From Percy?

Sure.

But not by busting him. Or even threatening to bust him. Kyle didn't know how or where or when Percy would be able to help, but Kyle sure as heck knew that the biggest-selling writer of all time didn't drop into your lap every day, so Kyle had better come up with some way of taking advantage of his newfound fortune. The same way he'd better take advantage of his friends.

Not Percy's friends.

Chad and Tyrone.

Kyle's friends. His best friends. His buddies. The three of them were already pretty much a team. So now they'd just be a different kind of team. A team to get his dad's book published. But that was the trouble. They were kids. Who'd ever listen to kids? Unless they acted undercover. Like ghosts. So no one would know. Not his dad. Not his mom. Not even the people who published the books.

What had Percy called himself?

Cynthia Marlow's agent?

Well, Kyle knew what agents did. They helped writers get their books published. Which Percy certainly did. Better than anyone who ever lived. Only Percy was an agent for a writer who didn't exist. Which meant Percy was undercover too. No, Percy was more than that. Percy was secret. Which was exactly what Kyle and Chad and Tyrone would be. They'd be agents. Secret agents.

"Hi, Kyle."

The voice didn't startle Kyle. He didn't jump. In fact he was happy to see Lucinda. Not that she had just gotten there. She'd been sitting on that park bench less than five feet away since Kyle and Shakespeare had arrived. Only Kyle hadn't noticed. Only this time Lucinda didn't get upset. Because this time she knew. Not about the secret agent stuff. She knew about Kyle's dad. Because Lucinda had overheard her mom talking with Mrs. Freeman who'd been talking with Mr. Dixon who'd seen Kyle's father load a whole bunch of boxes into a taxi after Kyle left for school.

So I take it back.

Lucinda was upset. But not for herself. She was upset for Kyle. So she came to the park. Because she knew Kyle always walked Shakespeare to the park. Because she wanted to tell Kyle she was sorry. Mostly because she was. But also because that was another thing you did when you had a mad crush on someone who didn't have a mad crush back. You went to see him when he was sad. And told him you were sorry. And left your sunglasses at home.

"Hi," Kyle said.

"I'm sorry about your dad," Lucinda said.

"Thanks," Kyle said.

Then neither of them said anything for a while. They just sat there. So close Lucinda could have reached over and patted his rooster hair. Though she didn't. She didn't dare. Since she'd never touched him before. And she was too scared to now. Or anxious. Or both.

Which Shakespeare must have felt. Or sensed. Because he pushed himself up. And tiptoed over. And did the unthinkable. At least as far as Kyle was concerned.

"He licked you!" Kyle cried.

"Duh!" Lucinda said.

"Shakespeare licked you!"

"You said that."

"He licked you!"

"Kyle, you're flipping me out!"

And he was. Sort of. I mean, he kept repeating himself, sure. But there was also that look in his eyes. The one Lucinda had never seen before. When he looked at her, at least. Or was it when he looked at her book?

That's right. Lucinda had brought a book. You know, to read. While she sat on the bench waiting for Kyle. Because Lucinda was a reader. A real reader. Someone who never went anywhere or did anything without at least one book to fall back on. That kind of a reader. Which was something Kyle had never noticed. Along with just about everything else he'd never noticed about Lucinda. Including her belly. Which, since she was still wearing the same T-shirt she'd worn that morning, Kyle was noticing now. Which Lucinda was noticing. And liked noticing. Though not for long. Since Kyle couldn't keep his eyes off the book.

"I was just saying—"

"That Shakespeare licked me. I know."

"You don't understand."

"What's to understand? That Shakespeare never licks anyone? Except you and Percy Percerville? And now me? That's no more strange than you taking your eyes off my stomach to stare at this silly romance novel I'm reading so I can see if it follows the horror story formula where the monster stalks the heroine to some secluded spot—preferably a castle with a moat around it or an upstairs bedroom closet. Only in *Once More from the Top* the monster is a slick, phony film director and the secluded spot is an on-location movie set."

"Huh?"

"Never mind."

"Do you always talk like that?"

"Only when I'm showing off."

"Well, you forgot something."

"What's that?"

"The name of the author."

"Cynthia Marlow? Why is she important?"

And so Kyle told her. Just like that. He opened his mouth, and the words came out rat-a-tat-tat so fast he couldn't stop, not even when he got to the part about the secret agents—which, five minutes before, he swore he'd never tell anyone but Chad or Tyrone.

Why Lucinda?

Because Shakespeare licked her hand. And Kyle noticed the book. And Lucinda went into her horror/

43

romance lecture. Which meant nothing to Kyle, of course. Except that Lucinda was smart. And knew about books. Though catching a glimpse of Lucinda's belly hadn't hurt things either. Since it took her out of the kid category. And placed her into what category Kyle wasn't sure. But certainly smack dab into the middle of the secret agents. If that was what she wanted. Though Kyle couldn't tell. Since she kept that deadpan look on her face right up until his very last sentence.

"No way!" Lucinda cried.

"You mean you won't do it?" Kyle said.

"Of course I'll do it!" Lucinda said. "I'm just saying I can't believe Percy Percerville is Cynthia Marlow."

Chapter 9

It didn't feel right. Not to Kyle. When you and your buddies were about to make a secret pact, you should have been out in the woods under a full moon around a campfire. Plus, you should have been wearing a cloak. You know, with a hood. To cast your face in shadows. While you waited. And listened. For a lone wolf to howl. Before you picked up a sharp rock or piece of flint. And pricked your finger. So you could sign your name in blood.

But there weren't any woods on Twentieth Street. Or wolves. And, yeah, you might have been able to find a monk and talk him into lending you his cloak. But you could get tossed into juvenile detention for walking around with a sharp rock in your pocket. And who knows what might happen if you started a campfire?

So okay. So you might be able to set up some candles in a bedroom or basement and prick your finger with some kind of secret pact safety pin or something, but what would happen if a parent walked in?

Nope.

No way.

It couldn't be in anyone's house. And Twentieth Street had no back alleys. Same with Eighth and Ninth Avenues. And Central Park was too far away. What Kyle and his friends needed was a clubhouse. Or an abandoned building. But there were none. Not safe, anyway. So they met at a soda fountain. That's right. Only it wasn't *really* a soda fountain. Since there wasn't any soda. Or even ice cream.

On the southwest corner of Twenty-first Street and Ninth Avenue stood a one-story building shaped like (I swear) a caboose. Not a red caboose. A silver caboose. Slick. Sleek. Like a rocket ship with wheels. Which it had. Fake wheels on fake tracks under a blue neon sign that flashed:

THE TOFU TUTTI-FRUTTI

You think I'm kidding, but at eight o'clock that night there they were: Kyle, Lucinda, Chad Simon, and Tyrone Brown. Crammed into a back booth. Their butts squeaking on the vinyl cushions. Their elbows sticking to the Formica tabletop. Chad was punching numbers on the jukebox. Any numbers. Since it was free. And since the only songs it played were cha-cha and doo-wop and rock and roll that was old when your parents were your age. The specialty of the house was whipped soybeans and dehydrated raspberry powder. Served in real glass glasses. Scooped with real metal spoons. The place was so retro it was almost cool. Until, of course, you took that first bite.

"Yuk!" said Chad.

"Shut up!" said Tyrone.

"No, you shut up!" said Chad.

"No, you shut up!" said Tyrone.

If Kyle hadn't felt right before, you can imagine how he felt now. Secret pacts were supposed to be solemn and mysterious. Not some goofball sideshow with two of the three stooges about to start a food fight. But, like I said, Chad and Tyrone were Kyle's best friends. And Tyrone's parents owned the place. And Tyrone had to work that night. So it was either the Tofu Tutti-Frutti or nothing.

"How come *she's* here?" said Chad.

"How come *you're* here?" said Tyrone.

"Ooh! Snappy comeback!"

"*Ooh* yourself!"

In case you can't tell, Chad and Tyrone weren't exactly crazy about each other. Especially if there was a girl around. Which wasn't that often. Since girls didn't exactly flock to these two. Especially Chad. Who was one of those totally obnoxious friends we all seem to have but are never exactly sure why. No, that's not true. We know. And so did Kyle.

You see, Chad had been Kyle's first friend, way, way back in first grade. Mr. Pepe. That was their teacher. Mr. Pepe was the first adult outside of Kyle's parents who didn't speak to Kyle as if he were a kid. That was Mr. Pepe for you. A forty-year-old man in a button-down white shirt and paisley tie, who treated every single seven-year-old lucky enough to set foot inside his classroom as the unique and special individual he or she deserved to be. Even if his desk was a mess (like Kyle's). Or if he always colored inside the lines (like Chad).

"Future citizens!" Mr. Pepe announced each morning right after the Pledge of Allegiance. "Wisdom is what we seek! Respect is what we demand! For ourselves, to be sure! But, just as importantly, for our classmates!"

It never failed. Kyle couldn't think of those words without smiling to himself. And feeling good about himself. And respecting himself. But it didn't end there, of course. Because that was only half of Mr. Pepe's lesson. The other half was Kyle's fellow future citizens—a category that included you-know-who and his sharpened crayons—making it nearly impossible for Kyle not to respect or feel good about or even like Chad Simon.

Plus, he was loyal.

Chad, I mean.

I mean, he'd never taken sides with anyone against Kyle. Not once. Not ever. Oh, sure, *Chad* could call Kyle a lame-o or a loser or any of those other lovely terms boys call other boys, but let someone else get in Kyle's face, and there was Chad. With a blow-by-blow description. Of how much money he'd be making in the future. Off you. After he became a plastic surgeon. Just like his dad.

"Five grand to fix that nose. Another three-point-five to suck that fat out of your thighs."

You get the picture. So did Tyrone. Who moved to Twenty-second Street *after* first grade. Which meant Tyrone never heard Mr. Pepe's respect speech. Which meant Tyrone never figured out why Kyle hung around Chad more than five seconds. Though Tyrone never asked. Why? Because Tyrone didn't have the guts. Which was the main reason girls didn't hang out with him either. Because Tyrone wasn't exactly filled with self-confidence.

Not because of the usual reasons.

Since Tyrone was tall enough. And good-looking enough. And coordinated enough. And way, way more than smart enough. But the one thing Tyrone liked to do more than anything else was sing. Which he did. All the time. Except he sang opera. Yep. That's right. Picture a kid who wasn't the least bit interested in rap or hip-hop or even rock and roll, but spent at least two hours a day, every day, practicing "Mi-mi-mi-mi-mi! Lo-lo-lo-lo-lo!"

and you might see why some of the less sophisticated members of Tyrone's peer group gave him the razz every once in a while. Which may have been a silly reason for Tyrone to lack self-confidence. But then, no one ever said boys weren't silly.

Certainly not girls.

Which brings us back to Lucinda. Who, of course, was the *she* Chad had been referring to when he said, "How come *she's* here?" Which might have caused some girls to squirm on their vinyl cushions. Though Lucinda wasn't one of them. Not that she snapped back. Not right away. First she had to swallow a particularly tasteless chunk of either tutti or frutti—she wasn't sure which—before she laid her metal spoon on the Formica tabletop, folded her arms across her chest, and locked those laser beam eyes of hers onto Chad Simon's famous smirk.

"I'm here because Kyle asked me," she said. "And if you don't like it, maybe you and I can step outside."

These were the first words Lucinda had spoken in Chad and Tyrone's presence. And she said them softly. Almost sweetly. I say *almost* because *sweet* was the last word any of the boys in that booth would have used to describe Lucinda's tone. You know the way your throat catches and your eyes blink when you try to be cool but don't quite pull it off? Well, none of that happened here. Every word came out clear. And steady. So steady that

Tyrone was certain he saw Chad's Adam's apple bob. Like a pogo stick. As if Chad were trying to gulp, but couldn't.

You see, Chad was big. Not fat—soft. If you pushed your finger into his belly, your finger would probably disappear. No one knew for sure. No one tried. Because, like I said, Chad was big. So, besides being obnoxious, Chad was also a bully. A verbal bully. He said things. Not mean things. It was more the *way* he said them. Like he was always right. And no one ever called him on it. I mean, Tyrone tried. Up to a point. But Tyrone always backed down. So the only one who ever really stood up to Chad was Kyle. And even he never threatened to fight. Which was obviously what Lucinda was threatening. Which, Tyrone was pleased to notice, seemed to fluster Chad so badly he never got around to mentioning how much it would one day cost her to chisel her cheekbones.

"Stop it!" cried Kyle. "I called you here because I'm in trouble! Because I need your help! But if all you're going to do is argue, then I'll leave! Right now! And do it all myself!"

Silence.

Total.

Sure, there were other customers at other tables, but every one of them picked that moment to shut up too. Chad? Tyrone? Lucinda? All three turned beet red and stared at the table. Because Kyle was right. He was in trouble. He needed their help. And all they'd been doing was thinking of themselves. So now they were ashamed. Which, oddly enough, was good. Good for Kyle, at least. Since it put even more pressure on them. So much so that, Kyle figured, there was no way they could say no to him now.

"Okay," Kyle said. "I'm going to tell you a secret. But before I do, I need you to promise me something. I need you to swear."

"We swear!" they said.

"I haven't told you what you're supposed to swear to yet," Kyle said.

"Oh," they said.

"This secret," Kyle said. "No one else can know. *No one!* Understand?"

They nodded.

"Swear it."

"We swear."

"Clasp your right hands in the middle of the table."

They clasped their right hands in the middle of the table.

"Swear it."

"We swear."

"Close your eyes."

They closed their eyes.

"Picture the worst thing that could ever happen to you."

They pictured the worst thing that could ever happen to them.

"Swear it."

"We swear."

"I will never break this sacred pact," Kyle said.

"We will never break this sacred pact," they repeated.

"Swear it."

"We swear."

"Good," Kyle said.

And nodded. Once. And put his hand on top of their hands.

"You are now secret agents," he said. "Just like me."

Chapter 10

It was midnight. Kyle slipped out of bed and felt a shiver shoot up the back of his legs as his feet touched the hardwood floor. The house was chilly. But not that chilly. Kyle shivered because he was scared. Scared of what he was about to do. Scared because he was going to have to do it alone. Because that was the deal. Tonight the secret agents were going to make their first move. Only tonight was a one-man job. That was the way Kyle had explained it to the secret agents. And they had agreed. Or at least Chad and Tyrone had agreed.

Lucinda?

Nope.

She hadn't agreed to anything. She'd sat on her hands and kept her mouth clamped shut. Which Kyle had noticed. You bet he'd noticed. Though he hadn't said anything. No one had. Except Tyrone. But all he'd said was, "Good luck." Which Kyle may not have needed.

Or at least not as much.

If his dad had left his PC behind.

But his dad hadn't. He'd taken his PC and his chair

and the books on his bookshelves and all the rest of the stuff from his office and moved them to the room above the Open Book. Except for the desk. And the old-man photograph of Ernest Hemingway with his white beard. The desk was too big to move in a taxi. And the photograph covered the wall safe.

Which told Kyle two things: First, the manuscript was still in the desk, or the drawers would be unlocked. And second, the backup disk was still in the wall safe, or the photograph would be gone.

Which meant Tyrone had been right.

Kyle needed all the good luck he could get. Because Kyle couldn't simply hack into his dad's PC and read the book. He had to break into his dad's desk. Which looked more like a solid oak fortress than a place where you sat down and dreamed up a story. It was an old desk. Really old. And ugly. With a cubbyhole a grown man could barely slide his knees under, and two drawers to the right of the cubbyhole that locked and unlocked using the same lock.

So why did Kyle have to break into them now?

Tonight?

Because Kyle's mom had told Kyle that tomorrow his dad would be coming with a pickup truck to take the desk to the Open Book.

That was what Kyle had explained to the secret agents. He'd told them tonight was the night. His only chance. Which sounded fine then. Exciting even. But sounded a whole lot different now. Alone. In the dark. Tiptoeing into the room. His heart hammering. His legs going wobbly. His mom sound asleep two floors up.

Tap! Tap! Tap!

Kyle jumped. So high and so fast Shakespeare would have been proud.

Tap! Tap! Tap!

This time Kyle was ready for it. Sort of. And his first thought was that it had to be his mom. Her footsteps. That she was awake. And walking down the stairs. But her slippers didn't go *Tap! Tap! Tap!* Which sounded more like a knock than footsteps. No, not *like* a knock. It *was* a knock. Which didn't necessarily rule out his mom. Maybe she'd woken up. And read his mind. And was telling him not to touch his dad's desk in Morse code through her bedroom floorboards.

Tap! Tap! Tap!

But the taps weren't coming from above. They were coming from here. This floor. And they sounded more like knuckles on glass than wood. Which didn't make sense unless . . .

Tap! Tap! Tap!

Kyle nearly went into his kangaroo routine again. He didn't. His heart did his hopping for him. Because he turned. And stared. At the office window. And saw two eyes staring straight back at him.

Tap! Tap! Tap!

Fortunately Kyle had a strong heart. So it didn't blow a valve. Or flood a chamber. Or go on strike and stop beating altogether. Nor did Kyle faint. Nor scream. Nor run away. Nor do any of the thousand things that would cause him to crash into a wall or knock something onto the floor. Instead, he just stood there. Frozen. His mouth hanging open. His eyes popping out. Which made him look silly. That was for sure. But at least it didn't wake up his mother. And bring his secret agent society to a screeching halt.

Tap! Tap! Tap!

By now the tapping was getting old. At least to Kyle. And you can bet Lucinda agreed. Since she was the one peering in through the window and bruising her knuckles while she tried to convince herself that sometime before the sun came up, Kyle would surely have to close his mouth and put his eyes back inside their sockets and come to the back door and let her in.

Which, of course, was why she'd sat on her hands and kept her mouth clamped shut back at the Tofu Tutti-Frutti. She knew she'd never be able to stand it. That she'd have to do something—*anything*—besides stare at her ceiling all night long and picture Kyle in front of his dad's locked desk with his heart hammering and his legs going wobbly. And, no, it wasn't easy getting here. But I'm not going to spend a whole lot of time telling you how her stomach cramped when she cracked open her front door, or how creepy the school behind Kyle's house was in the middle of the night, or about the goose bumps up and down her back when she crawled by the security guard. Because you're probably more interested in why Kyle's dad was such a dope and left his manuscript behind in the first place.

Because you're right. It was dopey. But Kyle's dad figured his manuscript would be more protected locked up in his old office than sitting out in the open in his new apartment. Because the Parker family trusted one another. Kyle's dad was certain that neither Kyle's mom nor Kyle would ever go back on their word and read what they'd promised they'd never read. Which, of course, was what Lucinda figured Kyle would figure. And get a guilty conscience. And maybe even freeze. Which was only part of the reason she skinned her knee climbing the wall between the school and Kyle's teeny-tiny backyard.

Tap! Tap! Tap!

Okay. Okay. That's it. No more tapping. The synapses in Kyle's brain finally fired enough jolts to let him know it wasn't a burglar or a werewolf or his dad busting him cold. Maybe Kyle recognized Lucinda's eyes. Or her lips. Whatever. He did. Finally. And felt his heart slide out of his throat. Enough to give him the strength to lift his right leg. And move it forward. And do the same with his left. In what wasn't the smoothest walk you ever saw. But it got him to the back door. Which got Lucinda inside. Which was all that really mattered. Since, as Kyle was about to discover, he didn't have a clue how to open a locked desk. Which was the second reason Lucinda skinned her knee on that wall. Though she wasn't thinking that. Not at the moment. Instead, she was thinking about her mother's famous warning:

"No one likes a know-it-all, dear."

These may not have been the sweetest words Lucinda's mom ever whispered in Lucinda's ear. But two years ago they'd stopped Lucinda from telling her dad how to connect the wires to the woofers and tweeters of the stereo. Lucinda knew how to connect them, of course, because she'd read the manual. Which Lucinda's dad hadn't done. Which was why the Brandenburg Concertos sounded fuzzy.

The next day, when Lucinda and her mom were alone, Lucinda's mom told Lucinda she could now connect the wires correctly but never mention a word of it to her father. So Lucinda did. Knowing full well her dad would notice the difference in the sound and get mad. Or hurt. Or something. Except he didn't. Or, if he did, he kept it to himself. Which absolutely amazed Lucinda. But it also taught her a lesson. It taught her there was truth, sure. And honesty. And these were good things. Of course they were good. But there were also times when cold, hard facts were not as important as people's feelings.

So you can imagine Lucinda's dilemma as she watched Kyle twist a paper clip, then a screwdriver, then, finally, a bent fork one way and the other inside the Stamford lock that locked the top drawer of his dad's desk. Lucinda knew it was a Stamford because, like the woofer and tweeter manual, she'd read all about locks after she'd read a story about a safecracker when she was in the fourth grade.

So Lucinda knew that if the Stamford was old, really old, as old as his dad's desk looked, you didn't need to actually pick the lock. All you needed was something thin and firm—like a laminated library card—to slip into the slot between the top of the drawer and the drawer frame and then slide the card to the right. That would unhook the hook. Both hooks. Which would unlock the drawers. Which was what Kyle wanted to do. And Lucinda knew how to do. Only there was all that truth and feelings stuff Lucinda had to deal with, since the way Lucinda saw it, her mom was only part right when she whispered, "No one likes a know-it-all, dear," since her mom should have added, "especially a guy."

"Kyle?" Lucinda said.

Kyle didn't answer. Kyle was back to twisting the paper clip with his right hand. And jerking a flashlight with his left. And probably making a mark on the lock that his father could spot from across the street blindfolded. While Lucinda was just about to jump out of her skin watching Kyle bungle the whole thing. Plus, she hated the sound of her voice a moment ago when she'd said "Kyle" all mushy-gushy. Like Kyle was some delicate treasure you dare not drop or his self-esteem would shatter all over the floor. So Lucinda simply sucked in her breath, pulled her laminated library card out of her back-right pocket, gently pushed Kyle's hand aside, slipped the card into the slot, slid the card right, heard the click, and opened the top drawer.

"Cool," Kyle said.

And that was it. That was all he said. Not "Know-it-all," or "I was just about to do that," or "You think you're so smart, don't you?" He said, "Cool." And looked at her. Really looked at her. The way he looked at Shakespeare. Just for an instant. But an instant was enough to turn Lucinda's heart into thunder.

"What's wrong?" said Kyle.

"Nothing."

"You look upset."

"I'm not upset."

"Okay," said Kyle.

"Okay," said Lucinda.

"So where did you learn to do that?"

"Pick the lock?"

"Yeah, pick the lock. What did you think I meant?"

For a moment Lucinda thought he meant where did

she learn to put her hand over her heart to stop it from crashing out of her rib cage. Which should give you a pretty good idea of how flustered she was. Which made her even more flustered. Since the last thing she ever wanted to be was a girl who got flustered. Which made her wonder whether she really wanted to have a mad crush on Kyle Parker if it meant possible broken ribs every time he gave her his dog look. So she made a deal with herself. No more mad crush. She and Kyle were secret agents. With a plan. A plan to get Kyle's dad's book published. And that was it. Period. Forget all the other stuff. It would just get in the way.

"I read it in a book," she said.

She said it proud. She said it know-it-all. Since who cared what he thought about her now? Only Kyle was no longer paying that much attention. Because his eyes had shifted to the open desk drawer.

Chapter 11

Love in Autumn
by
Walter Parker

So okay. So Kyle's dad's name was nowhere near as odd as Percy Percerville. But let me tell you something. Walter had his moments. I mean, you met him. You know where he worked and how much he loved his son and what a great big dreamer he was. And that should give you a pretty good idea about his book, right? I mean, a book a guy wrote should be like the guy, right? At least sort of. At least in the same stratosphere. At least that's what you'd figure. Except if you lived to be a zillion years old you'd never be able to figure out what *Love in Autumn* was all about.

First off, the manuscript was thin. Like thirty pages tops. Which, as you might imagine, freaked Kyle out. All over the place. Though he didn't want to admit it. Or even think about it. As he jerked the pages out of the drawer. And checked again. But, no, that was it. The drawer was empty. There were no more pages.

So he swallowed.

Or tried to swallow.

And sat down on the floor. And clicked on his flashlight. And read the first page. And couldn't believe it. So he read it again. Only this time the words seemed to whirl around the page. Or maybe that was him. Maybe he was the one who was whirling. But he stopped. He steadied himself. And gulped down some air. And handed the page to Lucinda. Who read it right after him. And it kept on going just like that. Page after page. Minute after minute. For the next fifteen minutes.

He read.

Then she read.

He read.

Then she read.

The grandfather clock in the hallway chimed once, but they didn't hear it. A streak of lightning flashed outside the office back window, but they didn't see it. They just sat there. Cross-legged. Stone-faced. Without saying a word. Without glancing at each other. As if nothing else mattered. As if no world outside *Love in Autumn* even existed. And, still, neither Kyle nor Lucinda could have told you what those pages were about. Not if you promised them world peace. Not if you hung them upside down and pulled their finger-nails off one by one.

Oh, sure, they knew it was a love story. And the guy was named Dirk. And the girl was named Ginger. And he was poor. And she was rich. And they met in a sleazy Seattle nightclub. And he had tattoos and piercings. And she had a makeover and a pedicure. So they had this whole Romeo and Juliet thing going. Or maybe they didn't. Since who could tell? Since all they did was crash into each other on the dance floor then say, "Wow, man!" all night long.

"Yuk!" said Lucinda.

"Ditto," said Kyle.

Or he would have if he could have said anything. Which he couldn't. Since all he could do was drop the last fifteen pages on the floor and close his eyes and want to scream or hit himself on the knee with a ham-mer or do anything to stop the typhoon that had started whirling around inside his brain all over again.

I mean, his dad was what? Thirty-eight? And lived in New York City all his life? And grew up on Fleetwood Mac and the Eagles? And had never been west of the Mississippi River? So what gave him the bright idea that he could possibly know anything about the sleazy Seattle nightclub scene? Not that Kyle was the best reader who'd ever lived. Far from it. But he could tell—starting from the first sentence—when someone didn't know what he was talking about:

Dirk and Ginger met in the mosh pit,
slam dancing and sweating their way into each other's heart.

Every day for the past six years, Kyle's dad had come in here—into this office—and closed the door behind him. And that was it. That was all anyone heard from him for the next five hours. No bathroom breaks. No lunch breaks. No nothing. Until he finally stumbled out so exhausted it took him until the six o'clock news to get back to being Kyle's dad.

But who was his dad?

I mean, he always seemed normal enough. And never took off his clothes and danced up Eighth Avenue. Or yodeled in the backyard. Which, the way Kyle saw it, was pretty much the equivalent of "slam dancing and sweating their way into each other's heart." I mean, Kyle thought he was bummed out before. You know, when his mom told him his dad wasn't going to live with them anymore. But back then Kyle still had a glimmer of hope. He still believed his mom and dad could get back together.

Now?

Now Kyle had nothing. Since he knew in his gut no one would ever publish this stuff. And worse, much worse, Kyle had no idea what was going on in his dad's head. I mean, how or where or when did he ever come up with such a stupid idea in the first place?

"Wait!"

That was Lucinda. Whispering. Though it was the kind of whisper you could hear across the street. Not that Kyle cared. Not anymore. Let his mom hear. What was she going to stop now? Since there was no plan. Since there were no secret agents. Since there was no book.

"Wait!"

Lucinda again. A bit quieter this time. But no less intense. Because she was still staring at the pages Kyle had dropped onto the floor. No, not pages. The last page. She'd skipped forward. Which was a habit with her. Whenever she hated a book so much she knew she wasn't going to read the whole thing, she always skipped to the last page to see how it all turned out. Only this time the last page wasn't the last page. Not of the book, at least. Instead, it was a letter. From Michael Strum. Who was an editor at Wilden Publishers. Lucinda knew this for a fact because she'd already read the letter. Twice. And was just about to read it again. Out loud:

"Dear Mr. Parker:

It's always a thrill to run across an exciting new voice. Your witty dialogue and perfect pacing move the story toward its tragic conclusion with the sure hand of a master storyteller. There is absolutely nothing I can tell you to improve this book except to say the characters are just too old for today's market.

All I can ask is that you please try another stab at the story with younger characters in a different setting.

I will be waiting. And, believe me, I will not forget who you are.

> *Sincerely,*
> *Michael Strum."*

There had been other big moments in Kyle's life. Like the time he stood up to Hector Lopez in the fourth grade or kicked the winning soccer goal while his grandfather was still alive or got licked by Shakespeare for the first time. But this moment right here, right now, would always rate right up at the top. Not that anything major happened. The heavens didn't crack open. A voice didn't boom, *"Here's the step-by-step fool-proof way to get a book published!"* But as he sat on the floor and listened to Lucinda read Michael Strum's letter, it suddenly dawned on Kyle that his dad wasn't nuts after all.

"So this isn't the real manuscript!" he said.

"Nope."

"I don't get it."

"Neither do I," said Lucinda. "Unless these thirty pages are just some silly story to prove how stupid Michael Strum is!"

"Huh?"

"Your dad wrote *Love in Autumn*. Then he sent it to Michael Strum. Then Michael Strum wrote back this letter that says people who read aren't interested in old people. Which is stupid. At least, I think it's stupid. And I'm betting your dad thought it was stupid too. Which was why he wrote these pages. To show it really doesn't matter what you write but how you write it. Which your dad already knew. But wrote the thirty pages anyway to let off steam."

"Are you showing off again?" said Kyle.

"Probably," said Lucinda. "But that doesn't mean the real manuscript isn't around here somewhere."

And maybe she smiled.

And maybe Kyle smiled back.

Though neither was sure.

Since they were too busy butting heads as they made a lunge for the bottom desk drawer.

Chapter 12

Empty.

Nothing inside the drawer. Or anywhere else in the desk. No false bottoms. No secret compartments. Kyle and Lucinda knew. They checked. Which meant the manuscript was somewhere else. But where? That was the question. Which wasn't really much of a question. Since Kyle was already shining his flashlight on Ernest Hemingway's white beard and angry eyes.

Remember him?

The photograph?

The only other thing left in the room?

Kyle sure as heck did. He also remembered what was behind it. So the question wasn't really Where? But How? How were Kyle and Lucinda going to break into a wall safe—a combination wall safe—without knowing the combination?

"What's your dad's birthday?" said Lucinda.

"Excuse me?"

"The date? When was he born?"

"September sixth, nineteen sixty-six."

Lucinda took the photograph off the wall, placed it on the floor, blew onto her fingers (not for any reason— she'd just seen safecrackers in movies do this millions of times), and dialed:

Nine left. Six right. Sixty-six left.

Nothing.

She tried it in reverse.

Still nothing.

She tried spinning the lock past the zero between the first two numbers then the second two numbers then all three numbers at the same time.

Still nothing.

She tried Kyle's mother's birthday and Kyle's birthday the same way—the same amount of times and combinations as she'd tried with Kyle's father's birthday.

Still nothing.

The grandfather clock in the hallway chimed. Again just once. Only this time it meant it was 1 A.M. Meaning Kyle and Lucinda had been at this an hour. And Lucinda was exhausted. Or at least frustrated. And though she wasn't ready to say it out loud, pretty much ready to give up. But not Kyle. He wasn't sure why. Or how. But the more the birthday numbers failed the more razor sharp his mind became. Even after the last spin of the last date, when Lucinda tried the handle one last time.

And it still wouldn't budge.

"November fourteenth, nineteen eighty-nine," Kyle said.

Lucinda sighed.

That's it. That's all she did. She didn't shrug. She didn't shake her head. She didn't say a word. She let her sigh do her talking for her. But her sigh came in loud and clear. Her sigh said:

"No, Kyle. No good. The dates aren't working. I was wrong about the dates. Forget about the dates. And forget about me—the brainy kid across the street with freckles all over her face and maybe a cool belly, but who cares, since all she knows are books and books and more books and nothing about the real world and certainly nothing about combination locks, and I wouldn't blame you if you never gave me one of your dog looks ever again if you live to be a hundred and sixty-eight years old."

"November fourteenth, nineteen eighty-nine," Kyle repeated.

But Lucinda just stood there. Frozen. Like even if her mind wanted to move, her body refused. Which didn't stop Kyle. Who simply reached over and took hold of the dial and spun it eleven left. Then fourteen right. Then eighty-nine left. Then pulled the handle. Then heard the click.

That's right.

The click!

As in:

He did it!

He figured it out!

Kyle Parker. Master safecracker. Who boldly spun dials where no one had spun dials before.

"How . . . ," Lucinda started.

But she couldn't get any more words out.

So Kyle ran it down for her:

"The pages we just read are a love story. Which means the real manuscript is probably a love story too."

"So?" Lucinda said.

"So my parents met at the skating rink in Central Park on November fourteenth, nineteen eighty-nine," Kyle said.

He said it nonchalant.

Or tried to. It wasn't easy. Not with his insides going nuts. Because he did it! He figured it out! Which, of course, was way cool all by itself. But it was nothing compared to Lucinda's eyebrows shooting up. In surprise. And awe. The moment the lock clicked open. Which Kyle liked. Lucinda's eyebrows shooting up, I mean. He liked it a lot. Though he didn't say that. He didn't say anything. He let his eyes do his talking for him. Which were about the size of cantaloupes as he reached in and took hold of the 263-page manuscript neatly stacked inside the safe:

Love in Autumn
by
Walter Parker

Funny what words can do to you. I mean, reading by flashlight wasn't the smartest thing Kyle and Lucinda ever did for their eyes. Plus, their legs went to sleep from the knees down. Plus, their necks felt as if they'd been squeezed in a vise. But neither noticed. Not really. Not after they read Kyle's dad's first paragraph, where they met eighty-six-year-old Charlotte Patton and climbed aboard her wheelchair and took that ride. Down the ramp of the old-folks home. Along the cracked Bronx sidewalks and boarded-up storefronts. Through the glass door of the arboretum.

That's right. The door was made out of glass. Though it may as well have been pixie dust as far as Charlotte was concerned. Because the place was magic. Or at least enchanted. Because that was where she met Ben Rivers. Who was not a prince. But a retired gardener who could no longer see but only smell the roses he'd cared for all his life. Every day from August through October, Ben explained why the petals of the Chrysler Imperial were more delicate and fragrant than the American Beauty. And every day from August to October, Charlotte pretended she hadn't heard it all before.

They never kiss. They never hold hands. The only time they even hint at the love they have for each other is the last day in front of the roses when the pain shoots through Charlotte's chest and she tries to move her lips but can't, and Ben finds her face with his hands and brushes a strand of hair out of her eyes and says, "Me too, darling. Me too."

There wasn't enough time to read the whole book, of course. Kyle and Lucinda skipped two chapters and skimmed three more. But that didn't stop Kyle, at the end of the last sentence, from blinking back a tear, which was nothing compared to Lucinda. Who'd practically soaked the whole front of her T-shirt.

"It's wonderful!" she whispered. "I told you Michael Strum was stupid. I told you it didn't matter how old Charlotte Patton and Ben Rivers are or where they live or how they meet. Your father's book is better than anything Cynthia Marlow or Percy Percerville or whatever he wants to call himself ever thought about writing, and any editor who's not an idiot will know that in three and a half seconds if we ever get the manuscript into his—or her—hands."

"Shh!"

"I'm sorry. I got carried away."

"Shh!"

"Quit shushing me!"

"Shh!"

"I said quit—"

But that was all she said. Because Kyle clamped his hand over her mouth. Which didn't exactly thrill her. But it shut her up long enough so she could hear Kyle's mom's footsteps echoing down the stairs.

Which set Lucinda off.

In a blur.

A silent blur.

I mean, she had Kyle's dad's manuscript out of Kyle's hands and into the safe and the safe door shut and the handle locked and Ernest Hemingway's photograph back on the wall so fast Kyle barely had a chance to realize there wasn't any place for the two of them to hide. Not that he didn't look. But, as you already know, the only piece of furniture in the office was the desk. And, yeah, it was big. And he and Lucinda could crouch behind it. But what was the point? Since Kyle figured the only reason his mom was coming down the stairs in the first place was because she heard Lucinda and him messing around down there. So Kyle was just about to shuffle over to the door—hands out, wrists close together—and greet his mom with something stupid like "Okay. I give up. Cuff me." When Lucinda grabbed him by the arm, yanked him straight down, shoved him into the desk cubbyhole, and pushed herself in next to him.

"Shh!" she said.

And, yeah, it was dark. But not dark enough that Kyle couldn't see Lucinda's wise-guy smile. And, no, he didn't smile back. But not because he was angry. Amazed was more like it. At the speed with which she moved. At the way she didn't panic. At the fun she seemed to be having. But, most of all, Kyle was amazed at the way her hip felt digging into his hip. It was soft. And round. And pretty much the way you'd figure a girl's hip would feel.

Errrrrrrrr.

You know what that was. The office door. The office door *hinge* to be exact. Kyle could no longer hear his mom's footsteps. But that just meant she was already there. Inside the office. About to flip on the light. And ask him what he thought he was doing. And discover Lucinda in the cubbyhole next to him. And ground him until he left for college. And the next time he saw Lucinda she'd be married and have fifteen kids. So he figured he'd better enjoy her hip while he had this last chance.

"What am I going to do with you?" Kyle's mom said.

"Make me live with Dad?" Kyle was about to answer.

Except Lucinda's face was two inches in front of his face. And her finger was pressing against her lips. And her eyes were so wide he could almost hear them screaming, "Keep your big mouth shut!"

So he kept his big mouth shut. Which gave him enough time to realize what Lucinda had obviously already realized. That his mom hadn't flipped on the light. That the cubbyhole was on the opposite side of the desk from the door. That his mom couldn't see them unless she had X-ray vision. That the tone in her voice was the tone she used when she was fed up with Kyle's dad, not Kyle. Well, maybe Lucinda hadn't realized this last one, but she realized enough to shut Kyle up.

Thank goodness.

Chapter 13

"You didn't get caught?" cried Chad.

"Nope," said Kyle.

"All your mom did was talk to your dad?"

"Yep."

"Who wasn't there?"

"Uh-huh."

"And she didn't say anything to you?"

"Nope."

"And you *were* there?"

"Yep."

"So what did she talk about?"

"None of your business."

And it wasn't. It wasn't even Kyle's or Lucinda's business. Though they had been there. And Kyle could still hear his mom's voice crack when she said how tired she was waiting for the book to be finished. Tired of being alone. Because Kyle's dad had been gone long before he left the house.

Gone inside his book.

Which was when she stopped talking. And started pounding the desk. Which shook up Kyle. You bet it shook him up. Especially since his mom's fists were hitting that solid oak no more than three inches above his head.

But, in a way, that was also good for him.

If he hadn't been hiding in the cubbyhole, he may never have known his mom wasn't as cut-and-dry as she pretended to be. Plus, he may never have realized that sometimes when two people split up there doesn't have to be a bad guy. His dad didn't set out to write a book he couldn't stop writing or ever get published. And his mom didn't tell herself if he didn't do one or the other she couldn't live with him anymore. That was just the way it turned out. Which, of course, was what Kyle was hoping for. Because if it happened once, it could happen again.

Only this time in reverse.

"Then what did your mom do?" said Tyrone.

"She walked out of the room," said Kyle.

"And?" said Chad.

"And Lucinda and I waited until we thought she was asleep. And I took the disk out of the safe. And I snuck up to my room. And I made two more copies of the disk. And I snuck back downstairs. And I gave Lucinda a copy. And I put the original disk back inside the safe."

"You gave *her* a copy?" said Chad.

"She wanted one," said Kyle.

"You do *everything* she wants?" said Chad.

"Sure," said Kyle. "I'm going over to her house after school and iron her clothes."

"That's a joke, right?" said Chad.

"You're a joke," said Kyle.

"Did you kiss her?" said Tyrone.

"Huh?" said Kyle.

"Did you kiss her?" repeated Chad. "Voice wants to know if you kissed the freckle-faced little creep good night."

"Don't call me Voice!" said Tyrone.

"*'Don't call me Voice!'*" repeated Chad.

"Why would I want to kiss her?" said Kyle.

"Because she may have been stupid enough to let you," said Chad.

"You didn't call her stupid last night," said Tyrone.

"I didn't kiss her," said Kyle. "I couldn't. She was already gone."

Which was true.

She was.

By the time Kyle had turned around from putting the disk back inside the safe, Lucinda had vanished. Just like that. Poof! Not that Kyle would have kissed her. Or even thought about kissing her. Well, maybe that wasn't true.

Maybe he thought about it. But only for a second. Because the moment he did, his tongue stuck to the roof of his mouth. So he had stopped thinking about it. Until now. When Tyrone asked. And Kyle felt his tongue turn into superglue all over again. Only this time Kyle couldn't make himself stop thinking. And not just about the kiss. But also the way his heart felt as if it had dropped into his belly. Last night. When he turned around from the safe. And Lucinda had disappeared.

Bong!

Oh, yeah. I forgot to mention where and when this kissing conversation was taking place. It was at school. The next day. During gym class in the middle of a volley-ball game, to be exact. Which wasn't too bad when Kyle and Chad and Tyrone were actually talking. Because the three of them could talk and play ball at the same time. But all that changed the moment Kyle said, "She was already gone." And Chad and Tyrone shut up. And Kyle drifted off. And started thinking about his tongue and his belly and all the rest. Which was where the *Bong!* came in. I mean, Kyle may have been able to talk and play ball, but daydreaming was another thing altogether. Especially when Ted Stevens sent a spike dead center at the bridge of his nose.

"Yow!"

That was Kyle. Screaming, sure. But also hopping up

and down. First on one foot. Then the other. As he cupped both hands under his chin to catch the blood. Which was pouring out of his left nostril like a faucet.

His teammates?

They were shook up. You bet they were. But maybe not the way you'd expect. Especially Ruben Gomez.

"Nice going, Parker," he said, kicking the ball into the folded-up bleachers. "We lost."

Ruben Gomez was, by far, the coolest kid at Roosevelt High School. He was the best athlete. He was the best looking. He was probably the toughest. I say probably because he never had to prove it. Because everyone figured you'd have to be crazy to pick a fight with Ruben Gomez. He didn't cut his sideburns to the tops of his ears. He didn't wear leather or bandannas or baggy pants so low you could see two-thirds of his boxers. He wore cotton shirts and pleated slacks and kept his hair cut so short it practically dried before it got wet. It wasn't a buzz cut. It wasn't razzle-dazzle. There was nothing flashy about Ruben Gomez except his eyes. Which weren't flashy like Christmas tree ornaments. Just intense. Never blinking. Never turning away. Not in fear *or* disgust. Not that Kyle had ever seen. Not until the volleyball smashed him flush on the bridge of his nose.

Don't get me wrong. Ruben wasn't afraid or disgusted

by the sight of the blood. It was something else. You could hear it when he said, "We lost," and called Kyle "Parker" as if Ruben couldn't even bring himself to call Kyle by his first name. And, yeah, Ruben was the one who nicknamed Kyle "Chicken Legs." But Kyle *had* chicken legs. It was like a joke between them. Not a taunt. Not nasty. Ruben wasn't nasty. He was the kind of guy who was so cool he didn't need to knock you down to build himself up. Except it was even more than that. Ruben *liked* Kyle. Always had. Even stood up for him. Like two weeks before when Kyle struck out with the tying run on third, and Ruben told Teddy Mitchell and Marcel Yost to keep their big mouths shut.

So what was going on?

Kyle had no idea. Which was the worst. I mean, you can't fix what you don't know. And, of course, Kyle couldn't ask anybody. Since no one (not even Chad) dared talk to someone Ruben had just dissed. So Kyle spent the rest of the day alone. Just him and his blood and the cotton balls that the nurse jammed up his nose. The blood stopped flowing in last period geometry. But the daydreams never stopped. Not even close. From the moment Ruben spit out the words *We lost, Parker,* the daydreams locked onto Kyle's imagination like lasers. Only now they pretty much homed in on what a loser he was, and how there was no way Lucinda would ever dream of kissing him, and worst of all, how there was absolutely zero chance that he—some chicken-legged kid who couldn't even play volleyball—would ever come up with a way to get his dad's book published.

Isn't the imagination great?

Just when you need it most, it either goes on strike or acts like it doesn't know you or starts teasing you worse than your big brother the first time you wet the bed. Not that Kyle had a big brother, but you know what I mean. Kyle sure did. All through lunch and biology and right on through to the end of geometry, this wise-guy, know-it-all voice kept echoing inside Kyle's head so loud he couldn't believe the kids around him didn't cover their ears:

"Idiot!"

"Jerk!"

"Grow up!"

"Get real!"

With no letup. None. Not even after the last bell of the last class when Kyle thought he would finally make his getaway, but realized before he even hit Union Square there was no getting away from yourself. Which may seem kind of obvious, but sometimes we don't pay all that much attention to the obvious stuff. Like our parents. And the way we take them for granted until one of them isn't around. Which may sound a little melodramatic since Kyle's dad hadn't exactly joined the Dalai Lama in Tibet. But Kyle was feeling a little melo-dramatic at the moment. Especially after the day he'd just had. Was still having. Since he still couldn't figure out what he'd done or hadn't done to Ruben Gomez.

Though he was about to.

The moment he opened his front door.

Chapter 14

Brownstone houses are built up, not out. Oh, sure, they start off regular enough. When you walk through the front door, you walk into the living room. But the dining room and kitchen are on the second floor. And the master bedroom is on the third floor. And the rest of the bedrooms are on the fourth floor. In other words, if you turned a brownstone on its side, you'd pretty much get a picture of what a regular, one-story house would look like. Except, of course, it would be turned on its side.

Kyle's house, though, was weird even for a brownstone. Because the first floor wasn't just a living room. There was also an office in the back. But you already know about that. What you don't know about is the living room. Which, let me tell you, is worth knowing about. Not because the couch had so much wood and hardly any fabric that it would have been more at home on the Ohio prairie than the middle of Manhattan. Or because the cracked leather armchair and wicker rocker were so mismatched they looked like they might start a fistfight. Or even because the glass-topped coffee table, from a certain angle, reminded you of a spaceship. Nope. That stuff is only interesting if you're interested in furniture. What is worth knowing about Kyle's living room is that it was a mess.

As in totally.

Like a cyclone had hit it.

Two cyclones.

I mean, sure. Right after Kyle was born, Kyle's mom or dad may have given the place a quick once-over, so none of their stacks and stacks of magazines would topple over and crush their infant son. But no one had touched anything since. Because Mr. and Mrs. Parker may have been a lot of things, but they certainly weren't neatniks. Or claustrophobics. Because they couldn't have been either and spent more than three seconds in that living room. Or, at least, used to. You know, in the past. Before Kyle returned home from school that afternoon. And turned his key in the latch. And pushed open the front door.

Because the place was spotless.

That's right.

No dust. No dirt. No magazines piled so high you figured they had to be in the *Guinness Book of World Records*. Oh, sure, there were still magazines. But only the most recent issues arranged alphabetically on either side of the coffee table. The ash and soot in and around the fireplace were gone. The logs were actually stacked *inside* the log holder and not dumped in the corner like some gigantic game of pick-up sticks. The windows were washed. The screens were washed. The ledges were washed. The hardwood floor was waxed. The glass covering the painting of the bull next to the halogen floor lamp was so clean you could actually tell it was a painting of a bull.

Which, of course, was a shock to Kyle's system. But it had nothing at all to do with Ruben Gomez. Except the woman standing to the side of the cracked leather chair wearing a starched black dress, white apron, white hat, and white shoes so highly polished they made Kyle want to squint was Ruben Gomez's grandmother.

Tall.

Thin.

A little slumped at the shoulders.

But head held high and skin still as smooth as butter-scotch pudding.

Carmelita Gomez smiled, put down the crystal letter opener she was polishing, walked the six steps to the front door vestibule, and held out her hand in a combination of moves so graceful it looked like dolphins swimming or her grandson banking one off the glass.

"I'm Carmelita Gomez," she said.

"I know," Kyle said.

And he did. He'd seen her before. Plenty of times. But always way, way across the school gymnasium, sitting next to Ruben's mother and father and sister cheering for her grandson. Never here. In Kyle's house. Polishing the crystal letter opener. Smiling her grandmother's smile. And staring at Kyle with a look so penetrating it left no doubt where Ruben got his intensity.

"I'm Kyle," Kyle managed to say.

"I know," Mrs. Gomez said.

And she smiled again.

And Kyle tried to smile back.

But he didn't quite make it.

So, okay. So Kyle knew Mrs. Gomez was working for his mother. Which meant, in a way, Mrs. Gomez was working for him. So how come it felt the other way around? Not that he was working for her exactly. But that he wanted to please her. He wanted her to think that he was doing a good job. A good job at what, Kyle didn't have a clue. But a good job at something. Even if it was shaking her hand and saying hello. And not just because she was Ruben Gomez's grandmother. But because of how she made Kyle feel. With that smile of hers. And those eyes. Not that she was judging Kyle. She wasn't putting him through any kind of a test. More like she got it. She knew what he was thinking before he was even thinking it, so there was no use trying to pretend. Which, of course, made Kyle want to pretend even more.

"Your mother hired me to clean your house a couple

of times a month," Mrs. Gomez said. "She told me she forgot to tell you. She told me you'd be surprised."

"I guess you could say that," Kyle said.

"I thought I just did," Mrs. Gomez said.

"You're teasing me," Kyle said.

"Not very much," Mrs. Gomez said.

And she smiled again. Her no-judgment smile. And Kyle was thinking she could go on teasing him the rest of his life as long as she never stopped smiling. Though she did. Nothing drastic. No dark curtain suddenly descended over the scene. She simply scrunched up her lips and creased her eyebrows as if she were about to say something serious.

"My grandson goes to your school," she said.

"Ruben," Kyle said.

"He doesn't like it that I clean houses."

"Uh-huh."

"He's embarrassed. He's especially embarrassed I'm cleaning yours."

Which, of course, was what Kyle figured the moment he saw her standing next to the cracked leather chair. Because he recognized her. And, of course, he realized what she was doing. Which made him realize why Ruben acted the way he'd acted. Which was funny. Or ironic. Because at that very moment Kyle was embarrassed too. Not for Ruben. Kyle was embarrassed for himself. Because Mrs. Gomez was cleaning his house.

Which was embarrassing all by itself. But it was even more embarrassing that his house was such a mess.

The only one who wasn't embarrassed was Mrs. Gomez. Which, when you thought about it, was the most ironic of all. I mean, if anyone should have been embarrassed, it was her. She was the one cleaning up after other people. If that's the way you wanted to see it. Which was the way Ruben saw it. Though it wasn't the way Mrs. Gomez saw it at all. She considered herself a businesswoman. Filling a need. A big need. Which was what businesspeople—smart businesspeople—filled. She also liked it. The cleaning part. She liked making messy things neat. Plus, she was good at it. I don't mean okay. I don't mean pretty good. I mean no one was faster, worked harder, had more knowledge about cleansers and surfaces and utensils, or took more pride in her work than Mrs. Gomez.

Buzzzzz!

The doorbell. Or the door buzzer. Whatever you want to call it, someone was at Kyle's door.

"Guess who?" Mrs. Gomez said.

Kyle had no idea. Not even close. I mean, he knew it wasn't his mother. She wouldn't be home for another three hours. And it wasn't Lucinda. She wrote Kyle an e-mail that morning telling him that after school she was going to spy on Mercedes Henderson. And it wasn't Chad or Tyrone. They'd still be treating him like kryptonite because of Ruben. So Kyle didn't know. So he just shrugged. Which made him feel dopey. Especially since he wanted to please Mrs. Gomez. Who didn't smile this time. But winked. As she reached past him, took hold of the doorknob, and pulled it toward her. Which was when Kyle quit feeling dopey, at least. Though what he switched to didn't make him feel all that proud either. Because the moment the door cracked six inches, Kyle saw the white-hot eyes of Ruben Gomez staring straight back.

Chapter 15

Yeah, I know. I just mentioned Lucinda was spying on Mercedes Henderson then kept on going as if it was no big deal. Well, it was. As a matter of fact, it was about as big a deal as you can get. You see, when Lucinda snuck out on Kyle while he was putting the disk into his father's safe, she didn't go straight to sleep. Nope. In fact, she didn't go to sleep at all. She shot out of Kyle's front door, ran across the street, ducked inside her house, tiptoed up the stairs, slipped into her room, and flipped on her PC.

Because there is something else I haven't mentioned yet about Lucinda. She was a compulsive. Once she started something, it wasn't that she didn't *want* to stop. She *couldn't*. Not until it was finished. Done. Behind her. *Kaput!* That included books, conversations, shopping, connecting stereo speakers, and it certainly included getting *Love in Autumn* published. Which was what she was up to the moment she flipped on her PC. She was starting Phase II of the Secret Agent Pact.

How?

By reading.

Every Web site listed on every search her exhausted mind could dream up: books, publishers, agents. She cross-referenced. She ran backgrounds on specific editors at specific companies. She followed blind leads down dead-end alleys. She backtracked. She began again. With different editors at different companies on different Web sites: oldageromance.com, oldageromancebooks.com, oldageromancepublishing.com.

More blind leads.

More dead-end alleys.

More backtracking.

More beginning all over again.

By 4:30 her temples throbbed, her ankles turned prickly, and the backs of her knees broke out into beads of sweat. By 5:15 her left eyeball felt as if the blood vessels had burst. By 6:05 the candy canes she was sucking on stopped giving her that sugar rush. By 6:15 her brain locked. Or, at least, it looked like it did. Because she froze. Like a zombie. Her fingers didn't twitch. Her chest didn't heave. Her nose didn't wiggle. Sure, she still blinked every forty-five seconds or so. But, other than that, she was out cold.

Or was she?

Ring!

Her alarm.

Ring!

Just before her mom cracked open the door:

"Seven forty-five, honey. Time to get dressed and go to school."

So okay. So Lucinda's alarm and her mom's wake-up call might not seem all that related to oldageromance-publishing.com. But to Lucinda it was like one of those cartoons when the lightbulb clicks on over Bugs Bunny's head. Because it's funny how your mind works. Sort of the same principle as a star shining brighter when you see it out of the corner of your eye. The moment Lucinda was distracted, the moment she stopped looking at her problem dead on, all those "best day of the week to submit a manuscript" and "what publishing company published what kind of books" and "which editor was now working where" facts and figures she'd been cramming into her head suddenly switched from dead-end alleys into interconnected highways leading straight to the door of . . .

"Mercedes Henderson."

Lucinda whispered the name. And the chill that tingled up her backbone made her whisper it again.

"Mercedes Henderson."

It was like a chant. The sounds and syllables gliding off her tongue as her fingers dashed off the e-mail to Kyle:

Spying on Mercedes Henderson after school.

More later.

Lucinda

And, yeah, you might call that message a bit cryptic. Kyle certainly did. Not that he didn't know who Mercedes Henderson was. He would have had to be living on Mars not to.

At thirty-two Mercedes Elizabeth Henderson was one of the youngest senior editors in the history of Boykin Books. Not because her dad owned the place. (He didn't.) Or her mom was a movie star. (She wasn't.) But because Mercedes Henderson had the knack for spotting new talent. The last seven books she'd edited all sold over a million copies in hardcover. And the last two books, *I'm Yours* and *He Won My Heart,* had both won the National Book Award and had sixteen hardcover printings each in the first four months of publication.

But it was more than that.

Way more.

Mercedes Henderson had been on the cover of *People, Vanity Fair, Glamour, Entertainment Weekly, Premiere, Interview,* and *New York Magazine* so many times even the publicity department at Boykin Books had lost count. People who'd never heard of Stephen King or J. K. Rowling knew the shade of Mercedes Henderson's lip gloss. And that she lived in the penthouse of the apartment building where *Rosemary's Baby* was filmed. And had killed a charging rhinoceros in Kenya. And worked the pit crew with Paul Newman at the last Indianapolis 500. And wore navy (not black) Donna Karan pantsuits. And kept her hair punk-short by having it trimmed twice a week at Mr. Frederico's on Madison. And read manuscripts by unknown writers every morning from 7:15 to 9:45 soaking in her tub, sipping blackberry herbal iced tea.

You get the picture.

Lucinda sure did.

A book published with Mercedes Henderson as the editor meant instant blockbuster, a nationwide tour, a movie contract. It meant Lucinda would be a hero. Kyle Parker would fall down at her feet. Never mind Mercedes Henderson only championed one book a year out of the thousand she read. *Love in Autumn* was going to be that one. Lucinda knew it. She could feel it.

Almost.

That's right.

Almost.

I mean, Lucinda already knew *I'm Yours* and *He Won My Heart* were romantic and tragic and funny and about as close to *Love in Autumn* as you could get. Except the characters were way younger and had a lot more money. Which meant maybe they weren't all that close. Maybe Mercedes Henderson had the same attitude as Michael Strum. Maybe she wasn't interested in old people. Or poor people, for that matter. So maybe Lucinda was dead wrong about Mercedes Henderson. Though that tingling up Lucinda's backbone told her she wasn't. But, still, she had to make sure. She had to see what Mercedes Henderson was like. Really like. Not the PR stuff. Not the tabloid stuff. And, the way Lucinda saw it, there was only one real way to check out Mercedes Henderson.

By being a spy.

Which was fine with Lucinda. Cool, even. Except it meant she also had to lie. You see, up until this point, neither she nor Kyle had told one. Not outright. Not blatant. They'd broken a few rules. They'd snuck around here and there. They'd left a few things unsaid. But no one had asked them a direct question, so they hadn't been forced to make up a dishonest answer. Nor had they volunteered information they knew wasn't the truth. And, strange as it seems, it stayed that way. Even after Lucinda got home from school. And changed her clothes. And finished her cookies and milk. And flung her backpack over her shoulder.

"You have to do research?" her mom said.

"Yep," Lucinda said.

"Big project?"

"Yep."

"And you remember how to get to the library?"

"Yep."

So okay. So a case could be made that Lucinda had just lied. I'm betting Lucinda's mom would have made such a case. But Lucinda didn't say she was going to the library instead of Boykin Books. She never said she wasn't going to spy on Mercedes Henderson. She answered her mom's questions. Pure and simple. And I'm not saying that was a good thing. I'm not telling you to try it on your mom. I'm not even saying Lucinda wasn't *ready* to lie. All I'm saying is *technically* no lie was told here. Though I doubt you or I or anyone else could ever convince Lucinda's mom of that.

Did Lucinda feel guilty?

You bet.

Enough to stop her?

Not a chance.

She walked up Eighth Avenue to Twenty-third, crossed at the light, walked down the stairs to the subway in front of Al's Shoe Repair, and took the E train to Fifty-third Street and Fifth Avenue. And, yeah, it may seem odd that a kid would walk here and take the subway there and wander the New York streets alone. But Lucinda was a city girl. She had the subway map memorized. She knew Manhattan was a grid. You could plop her down anywhere on the island with only a mass transit card in her pocket, and she would beat you home. Plus, she knew where *never* to walk, what streets *never* to go near, and how *never* to make eye contact with anyone except a policeman. And, if none of that worked, she wore a whistle around her neck to blow if anyone got weird, and carried Mace in her right-front pocket if anyone got really weird.

Which she was happy to have now. She even pushed her fingers into her pocket to make sure the canister was there. Not that she was frightened. She looked at it more like a pacifier. Or a lucky rabbit's foot. Because Lucinda had walked to school and taken the subway to the library and the movies and even the children's zoo at Central Park so often she could have done it blindfolded. But, still, she was riding underground. All by herself. Beneath zillions of tons of earth and steel and concrete. And the wheels were roaring. And the brakes were screeching. And the car was jerking left. Then right. Then left again. And every time it jerked there was always an instant she wondered if this was going to be the one car in ten million that jumped the track. Mainly because the bald guy across the aisle kept opening his jacket and flashing his WE'RE ALL DEAD MEAT T-shirt in her face.

"FIGISISSORRISTISIST!"

That was the subway guy on the intercom announcing the next stop. Which pretty much sounded like the last stop. As a matter of fact, every announcement at every stop sounded exactly like the announcement at every other stop. Which, of course, no one with normal human ears could understand anyway. But there were also signs along the tiled wall. And, as the brakes screeched the train to a crawl, Lucinda made out the FIFTH AVENUE–FIFTY-THIRD STREET stop. Which, as you already know, was her stop. So she waited until the doors slid open, kept herself from taking one last glance at the bald-headed guy, stepped out onto the platform, and was hit by a blast of soot and moist, hot air.

New York.

It may have been the greatest city going, but it wasn't all that hot on your lungs. At least, that was what Lucinda was telling herself while she was also telling herself to keep her hands away from her face because all she would do was smear the soot and sweat around.

The climb up the subway steps was crowded and a little creepy. Nothing major. No one screaming, "I'll kill your mother!" or some guy with scabs all over his forehead begging for spare change. Just the usual subway smell and people who should have known better cutting in front of you to save that extra half second. Enough to make Lucinda happy when she finally hit the sidewalk, diagonally across the street from one of those pocket parks, this one with a huge chunk of the Berlin Wall and the coolest waterfall fountain you ever saw.

Honk!

Eeerrr!

"Watch where you're going!"

"You watch where you're going!"

Honk!

Eeerrr!

Honk!

That was the other thing about New York. You not only felt it and smelled it, but you also heard it. Everywhere you went, the city followed you. You could shut your door in the back room on the top floor of your brownstone on Twentieth Street, and still a taxi driver flying up Eighth Avenue like some Jedi warrior would bang on his horn or slam on his brakes just to remind you where you lived.

Which was why Lucinda didn't cover her ears. Or freak out. Like I said, she was a city girl. The horns honking and tires burning rubber were no different to her than some kid living in Tennessee listening to a babbling brook or a chirping chipmunk. She simply kept on the south side of Fifty-third Street and fell into lockstep with the rest of the folks headed east toward Fifth Avenue. And, yeah, the buildings were taller and the sidewalks more crowded than her neighborhood. And everyone carried briefcases and wore business suits and very serious shoes. But Lucinda just copied the guy coming toward her in the polka-dot bow tie: chin raised, shoulders squared, eyes dead ahead.

For forty-five steps.

That's right. Boykin Books was less than fifty yards

from the subway stop. Past the guy selling soft pretzels. Past the two other guys selling African masks. Past the whole crowd of guys watching another guy deal three bent cards on top of a cardboard box.

Wooosh!

Breezeways aren't called breezeways for no reason. This one connected Fifty-third and Fifty-second Streets and worked pretty much like a wind tunnel. Though Lucinda didn't mind it half as much as she would have if she were passing it in the middle of January. But it wasn't January. And the rush of cool air felt good. And just on the other side, halfway down the breezeway, was the Boykin Books lobby.

Lucinda took a deep breath. The smell of grease and salt from the pretzels calmed her. So did the sidewalk vibrating from the subway rumbling underneath. Because it reminded Lucinda one more time that, yeah, she may well have been up on Fifty-third Street, but this was still her city. Her home. Her turf. No intimidation. No fear. She could walk into that lobby. Get on that elevator. Find out what she had to find out about Mercedes Henderson. Even though she wasn't exactly sure what that was. But she'd know it when she saw it. Or heard it. And she'd see it or hear it today. This afternoon. Right now. And no one was going to stop her.

"Can I help you?"

Four words. None of them much by itself. But the

four put together stopped Lucinda cold. Because they came out of the mouth of the security guard for the Boykin Books Building. Which almost made Lucinda giggle. The name, I mean. Someone must have really liked that hard *B* sound. Or Mr. Boykin must have liked to see his name in gray marble. Because there was plenty of that, let me tell you—the floor, the desk, the wall behind the desk, the casings around the elevators, the sculpture of the opened book in front of the elevators. For a moment Lucinda wondered if the guard might have been marble too. Though he wasn't. At least not gray. At least not his uniform. Though, as far as getting by him and onto an elevator that would take her up to see or talk to or spy on Mercedes Henderson, Lucinda could tell by the security guard's square jaw he might as well have been made of marble.

What had Lucinda been thinking? That she'd walk right in? Ride right up? Hide behind the water cooler or something? Weren't there, like, a thousand million billion writers who wanted their books published? Wouldn't every single one of them like to see or talk to or spy on Mercedes Henderson? Didn't it make sense that someone with a square jaw would be standing guard in the lobby, ready to swat them away like flies?

Lucinda was ready to kick herself in the butt. Or wallop herself in the kneecap. Because she should have seen this coming. She should have been ready with a snappy comeback that would have whisked her right in. But she wasn't. She didn't. And so she hesitated. Which the security guard saw. You bet he saw. And now his jaw got even more square. And his left eye narrowed. As if he were telling her he'd seen her kind before.

"Take a walk, young lady," the eye was saying. "Out you go. Beat it. No Mercedes Henderson for you."

If Lucinda had been Shakespeare, she would have tucked her tail between her legs and scampered right out that revolving door. But she wasn't Shakespeare. And she was more furious with herself than frightened. So much so she squeezed her fists and ground her teeth and started silently screaming something like:

"Spy? Yeah, you're a spy! Why not just strap on some blinking lights? Or twirl one of those party twisters? Or just admit it. Just look the guard right in the eye and say, 'Hey, don't mind me. I'm just here to secretly eavesdrop on the most famous editor in the world!'"

Did it make her feel any better?

Nope.

But that little bit of sarcasm was just enough. Not for Lucinda to come up with anything clever to get her by the security guard. But it was enough to stall her. Enough to stop her from stomping out the door. Maybe for a second. Maybe two. Which was all it took for the elevator bell to ring. And for the doors to separate. And for Mercedes Henderson to appear. That's right.

Like one of those birds that pop out of a magician's hat.

Poof!

I swear. No puff of smoke. No applause from the rest of the folks in the lobby. But there may as well have been. It was as if everyone within fifty yards stopped breathing. And moving. And every single eye in every single head followed every single move Mercedes Henderson made.

Did she toss her hair?

Cock her eyebrows?

Glide?

Float?

Shove people aside who got in her way?

Uh-uh. She walked. Like a person. Like you or me. Maybe even more tentative than we might have walked. With her head down. Blinking. Keeping herself to herself. Not haughty. Not like she couldn't be bothered with the type of riffraff that would hang out in the Boykin Books Building lobby on a Friday afternoon. But almost as if she were lost. And certainly sad. Clutching her purse as if it were a life jacket.

She had no entourage. No one was walking in front of her or behind her or holding the door for her or whistling for a cab. It was only her. By herself. Pushing her own door open and turning left down the breeze-way. That's right. She was walking. Not riding. Because the moment she reached Fifty-second Street, she didn't head straight for the curb to raise her hand for a taxi or hop inside a limousine. She turned right. And kept walking. Straight for Fifth Avenue.

With Lucinda hot on her trail.

Not obvious. Nothing to raise the security guard's suspicions. Lucinda played it cool. Looking him dead in the eye and raising her eyebrows as if to say, "Oops! Wrong building!" then following Mercedes Henderson out the door. Only Lucinda followed slow. As if she had all the time in the world. As if the last thing she ever wanted to do was follow anyone. Especially Mercedes Henderson.

Did the security guard buy it?

Guess so. Since he didn't cry "Halt!" or come charging out after her and grab her by the shoulder. He just sat. And Lucinda walked. Dogging Mercedes Henderson's footsteps. Twenty-five steps behind.

And check it out:

No one noticed her. Not Lucinda. Of course no one noticed her. But not a single guy or gal brushing or driving or racing past had any idea the great Mercedes Henderson was strolling down Fifty-second Street and making a left onto Fifth Avenue. Outside the Boykin Books Building, it seemed Mercedes Henderson was just another hip New Yorker with short, short hair dressed totally in black.

That's right.

Donna Karan, sure. The cut and shape of the lapel told Lucinda that.

But not navy.

Black.

All black.

Which Lucinda picked up on. Way back. Back at the elevator. Part of Lucinda's brain was already going, "Hmm." Which put her smack dab in the middle of her spy-game mode. Which meant Lucinda noticed things. And not just fashion statements. She noticed Mercedes Henderson's whole demeanor. I mean, here was one of the most glamorous women on the planet passing the most glamorous stores on the planet, and, as far as Mercedes Henderson was concerned, she may as well have been passing an outlet mall.

Gucci?

Nothing.

Harry Winston?

Zero.

Versace?

Not even a glance.

She kept her head down. Her shoulders slouched. No swerving. No detours. And, except for a light or two, she certainly didn't stop. Mercedes Henderson walked as if she had to walk where she was walking, but that didn't mean she had to like it.

Lucinda?

Thrilled.

Sorry, but that's the way it is with most of us. We don't

always look past our own needs. Since it was obvious something not-so-hot was going on with Mercedes Henderson. And all Lucinda could think was: "Whoa! Something's up! Something big! And I'm just the girl to find out what!"

Except she didn't.

Find out, I mean.

Because Mercedes Henderson disappeared!

Poof!

Just like that. Like that same bird popping out of that same magician's hat, only this time in reverse.

Here's how:

A young woman in a white uniform walking an old man with a tube sticking out of his nose were right in front of Lucinda. And, sure, Lucinda could have slipped past them easy enough, but they were a perfect shield in case Mercedes Henderson ever turned around. Perfect, that is, until the old man stutter-stepped to a stop so he could gnaw on his gums and stare at this display window with a slinky mannequin wearing a fake leopard-skin hat and a hot-pink leather dress cut eight inches above her plastic knees. Which meant Lucinda was stuck. Boxed in. By the display window on one side and a pregnant woman pushing a baby stroller on the other.

Five seconds.

That was all the time it took for Lucinda to wait for the stroller to pass, then cut around the pregnant woman. But those five seconds were enough. Mercedes Henderson had vanished.

Into thin air?

Nope.

Into St. Patrick's Cathedral.

Had to be. No question. It was the only building on the east side of Fifth Avenue between Fifty-first and Fiftieth Streets. That's right. It covered the whole block stretching all the way to Madison Avenue. Oh, sure, Mercedes Henderson might have ducked into the London Tobacconist or the B & B Delicatessen. Which were on the north side of Fifty-first Street. But Mercedes Henderson didn't smoke. Nor did she look like she was in the mood for pastrami on rye. And remember, she was wearing black. Which the spy in Lucinda remembered. Especially when she saw the dozens of other men and women all in black walking up the marble steps through the shadow of the matching towers and slipping in the side door.

Philip Harris
1928–2004
Memorial service: Friday, June 11
3:00 P.M.

Unlike Kyle, who'd taken at least ten seconds to figure out who Cynthia Marlow was, Lucinda knew the name Philip Harris the instant she read the announcement at the bottom of the cathedral steps. Editor in chief at Boykin Books for the past thirty-seven years, Philip Harris had not only been Mercedes Henderson's boss, but also her exact opposite.

Soft-spoken, shy, pretty much a ghost-about-town, Philip Harris had always believed the writer was the star. He never gave interviews. He never appeared on *Oprah* or Leno or Letterman. He was never quoted in the *New York Times*. He never even had his photograph taken. Well, that's not true. In 1981 a lone member of the paparazzi caught him sitting on a bench in Central Park talking to Shel Silverstein (about *A Light in the Attic,* no doubt). You could tell it was Philip Harris. He was wearing the same hat he'd been wearing to work every day since Harry Truman was president. Until five days ago. When Philip Harris took his hat off to catch a catnap going home on the downtown IRT and never opened his eyes again.

The tingle that had shot up Lucinda's backbone before did it again. Only this time it didn't pump her up. This time it gave her the creeps. Had she flipped out? Had her brain turned to mush? Philip Harris was the only old guy in Mercedes Henderson's professional life, and every newspaper and magazine article reprinted on the Internet said they hated each other! Pretty important fact to leave out of the equation, don't you think? I mean, fat chance Mercedes Henderson would ever be interested in *Love in Autumn*. You might as well ask her if she'd like to trade in her pantsuits for bell bottoms and love beads.

Which, of course, should have stopped Lucinda in her tracks.

But it didn't.

She crashed the funeral anyway.

Oh, sure, she told herself it was a waste of time. Not to mention insensitive and tasteless. I mean, would you want a spy at your funeral? But she didn't care. She didn't even slow down. Well, that's not true. She hung back. She waited. But only until she spotted a couple who looked as though they could have been her parents. And then she joined them. Or, at least, she walked close enough for the cathedral's guard to think they were together. Because he must have. Because she marched right up those marble stairs and straight through the side door, backpack and all, and the guard never so much as blinked.

"Do you think she'll speak?"

"She wouldn't dare."

"What's she doing here anyway?"

"Dancing on the grave."

Lucinda wasn't eavesdropping. The two old ladies who said this stuff said it so loud Lucinda would have heard it even if she'd covered her ears and hummed "Onward Christian Soldiers." Nor did Lucinda have any doubt who the "she" was. Not that Lucinda could see Mercedes Henderson. The cathedral was too big. There were too many people. But who else would it be? Philip Harris didn't have another enemy. Not a public one, anyway. Which, of course, only made the tingle up and down Lucinda's backbone tingle even more.

"She's sitting next to the priest!"

"No!"

"Yes!"

"How can you see?"

"There?"

"Where?"

"There."

Lucinda followed the old woman's crooked finger and discovered she *wasn't* pointing at Mercedes Henderson. Not exactly. I mean, it *was* Mercedes Henderson. But not in person. It was Mercedes Henderson on a television screen. That's right. You heard me. On the outside of every column lining the nave was a twenty-eight-inch Trinitron providing the folks whose vision was blocked with a play-by-play rundown of what was happening up at the altar. Which, at that moment, happened to be the priest nodding once, placing his hand on Mercedes Henderson's shoulder, then standing. Which must have been the cue. Because the moment he stood, the organ started echoing off the walls of the cathedral.

Philip Harris may have been soft-spoken and shy, but

that didn't mean he didn't have friends. Hundreds. Thousands. I mean, the pews in St. Patrick's practically took up a square city block, and every inch of them was filled. So were the side aisles. So was just about everywhere else Lucinda tried to move but couldn't. She managed to push and squirm her way up to the back of the pews, but that was as far as she could get. Which was about the time she realized that the TV sets on the columns may have been tacky, but if it wasn't for the one right in front of her, the only human faces she would have been able to see were the statues of Peter and Paul at the top of the great bronze doors at the back of the cathedral.

"Let us pray."

And the priest did. Only Lucinda didn't listen. Instead she glanced above the bronze doors and saw the rose window for the first time. And, yeah, it was big. Twenty-six feet in diameter. And designed by Charles Connick. One of the great stained glass guys of all time. Which hadn't meant all that much to Lucinda when she'd read it during her great-places-of-worship phase four years ago. But now. Right now. With the blues and reds backlit by the sunlight, the beauty caught Lucinda so off guard it felt as if her esophagus had suddenly shrunk and her capillaries had stopped pushing blood into her brain.

"Welcome."

The voice brought her back. The female voice. Mercedes Henderson's female voice. How the priest had left the pulpit and Mercedes Henderson had taken his place Lucinda had been too far gone into Rose Window Land to know. But the priest had. And Mercedes Henderson did. And she was now staring out over the congregation. The *hushed* congregation. Not that you could have heard a pin drop. Because you couldn't. Because nobody would have dropped one. Because everyone was frozen. Even the two old women who had called Mercedes Henderson *she* back at the cathedral side door. They had used their canes to beat their way to the foot of the nave. Where they now leaned forward. Their hearing aids turned up full blast. Their mouths curling into snarls. Ready to bite someone in the throat at the first nasty syllable to seep out of Mercedes Henderson's sin-red lips.

Chapter 16

"You did what?" cried Kyle.

"You heard me," said Lucinda.

"You submitted *Love in Autumn* for publication to Mercedes Henderson at Boykin Books?"

"Yep."

"Who's this?" said Ruben.

"I didn't know you had company," said Lucinda.

"What's your name?" said Ruben.

"Never mind," said Kyle.

"Never mind?" said Lucinda.

If you think you're confused, you should have seen Ruben. He'd been at Kyle's house maybe five minutes. And, no, he hadn't said anything. Since all he could think of was, "Next time, lower your head, and maybe you'll butt the ball over the net." Which didn't seem appropriate. Since you didn't get mad at someone for not being coordinated. Unless you were a jerk. Which Ruben wasn't. But that didn't make him any less mad. At his grandmother because she cleaned houses. At Kyle because Ruben's grandmother cleaned his house.

At himself because he got mad at his grandmother in the first place.

But just because Lucinda hadn't seen him didn't mean he was hiding. He'd just been sitting in the cracked leather chair when the doorbell rang and in walked the cutest girl since Lisa Bonet on the *Cosby* reruns. No lie. You see, Ruben hadn't grown up with Lucinda. She wasn't the little kid across the street who couldn't shoot hoops or kick a ball out of her shadow. She was new. Brand-new. And tough. And looked Kyle dead in the eye. And didn't back down. Plus, she ignored Ruben. That's right. Even after she realized he was there, she acted as if he were background noise. Which hadn't happened to Ruben since his first slam dunk.

"I'm Ruben," he said.

"Duh," Lucinda said.

Ruben's eyes went wide.

"Oh, please!" Lucinda said. "Ruben Garcia Gomez. The Garcia comes from your grandfather. Eighteen points, six assists, eleven rebounds, four steals per game through Regionals. Now, if you don't mind, Kyle and I are having a conversation."

Forget Ruben. Whose knees practically buckled he was so smitten. The surprise here was Mrs. Gomez. Halfway up the stairs. Where she'd stopped after she'd pretended to leave Kyle and Ruben alone. Which meant she'd caught every word Lucinda said. And smiled to herself that someone other than Ruben's parents had the guts to talk to her grandson as if he were human and not some majestic being you were supposed to bow down in front of and worship. But that wasn't the reason she had to grab hold of the railing to balance herself. It was when Mrs. Gomez heard Lucinda say she'd submitted *Love in Autumn* to Mercedes Henderson that Mrs. Gomez's knees turned almost as wobbly as her grandson's.

"We don't need the Secret Agent Pact!" Lucinda said. "Or a plan! Mercedes Henderson will publish the book! I guarantee it one hundred percent!"

Yeah, I know. How in the world could those five sentences turn anyone's knees wobbly? Except maybe Kyle's. Who felt the kind of sickness you feel in the pit of your stomach when you realize all your hopes and dreams are like those soap bubbles that pop into thin air.

"Let me get this straight," he said, doing his best to keep his voice even. "You gave a copy of the manuscript to Mercedes Henderson."

"Not her exactly," Lucinda said. "I gave it to the security guard at the Boykin Books Building. But I put Mercedes Henderson's name on the envelope."

Kyle didn't answer. He said nothing. Zero. Maybe he swallowed. Maybe he wasn't able to swallow. But he certainly gritted his teeth. And breathed through his nose. And counted to ten. And when that didn't work he counted to ten again. Which calmed him. Slightly. Enough to make him realize that Lucinda hadn't given *Love in Autumn* to the security guard to be mean. Or stupid. I mean, Kyle could tell by the look on her face that she thought she'd done the exact right thing.

And Kyle could sympathize.

Big-time.

Because, hey, this was Lucinda. The only person he'd told about Percy Percerville and Cynthia Marlow. Which may not sound all that related. But think about it. I mean, he didn't tell Chad. He didn't even *think* about telling Chad. I mean, ten thousand dollars? Chad would have turned his mother in for ten thousand dollars. And if Kyle couldn't tell Chad, it didn't seem right to tell Tyrone.

So he didn't.

He told Lucinda.

Why?

Because he trusted her.

Not to do the right thing. But to *try* to do the right thing. Which was why he didn't want to argue with her. Not now. Maybe not ever. So he counted to ten one more time until, finally, he calmed down to the point where he could say two words in a row without turning them into Scud missiles. Though what he said wasn't exactly what Lucinda had been hoping to hear.

"I've got to walk Shakespeare," he said.

And that was it.

He was gone.

And, no, he didn't stomp across the room. Or slam the door. But he was gone just the same. Leaving Lucinda with a lump in her throat the size of an avocado pit and Ruben with so many questions his tongue felt like a detonator switch.

"What—," he started.

But stopped as soon as he saw the look in Lucinda's eyes.

"You better sit down," he said.

And took her arm. And guided her over to the couch. And, yeah, she stumbled. Once. On the fringe of the rug. But Ruben held on tight until the backs of her knees touched the front of the corduroy cushion.

"Sorry," she managed to mumble.

Ruben shrugged.

"You must think I'm a ditz."

Ruben shrugged again.

"I'm not."

This time Ruben just looked at her.

"Well, maybe I am."

Lucinda barely got the words out before she burst out laughing. Not giggling. Not putting her fingers over her lips and going "tee-hee-hee." She gripped her stomach with her forearms. She doubled over. She snorted. She practically rolled off the couch.

Why?

No idea. I mean, she didn't know. But that just made it even more funny. Which made her laugh harder. Which made her feel better. Which made her want to talk. As a matter of fact, it made it impossible for her *not* to talk. Which Ruben picked up on. And sat back down on the cracked leather chair. And clasped his hands together. And put his elbows on his knees. And leaned forward. And waited.

Until the floodgates opened.

Of course, Lucinda skipped the part about Kyle's mom and dad splitting up and Percy Percerville being Cynthia Marlow. Since it wasn't any of her business to tell either story. Which she knew. The same way she knew it wasn't really any of her business to tell the rest. But she'd been so excited by what she'd discovered at St. Patrick's Cathedral, and so let down by Kyle's reaction, that she had to tell someone or her brain might have gone nuclear and splattered her skull all over the living-room ceiling. Which, of course, was exactly how she sounded. Because the words came shooting out of her mouth rat-a-tat-tat so fast Ruben had to cut her off.

"Slow down!" he said. "Take a deep breath. Okay. Now, tell me again. Who was this dead guy?"

"Her mentor!" Lucinda cried. "Editor in chief at Boykin Books! Don't you see? Don't you get it? That's what's so ironic. They were supposed to have been enemies! They were supposed to have hated each other! But they weren't! They didn't! Not even close! Mercedes Henderson got up in front of three thousand people and said she owed Philip Harris everything! Her first bestseller? *The Night Never Stops*? She was going to turn it down. Flat out. Send it back. Reject it. But Philip Harris called her into his office, sat her down, talked to her for over two hours. Not yelled at her. Not scolded her. But talked to her about books. And publishing. And told her how much easier and safer it was to say no to a new author. That saying yes was putting yourself out on a limb. 'Though what better place is there to be?' she said he said. Which hit Mercedes Henderson in her soul. And she went right home and reread *The Night Never Stops*. And called the author at one thirty in the morning. And told him what was wonderful about his book and what needed work. Which, Mercedes Henderson said, was the moment she became a real editor."

Poor Ruben. He could tell you how to pick and roll or set a screen or even hit a three pointer with two seconds left in overtime, but all this book stuff made about as much sense as Mr. Baker in physics explaining how the faster you travel the more time slows down. I mean, he wanted to understand. He wanted to be excited. Because Lucinda was excited. So if he was excited—or at least acted excited—then maybe Lucinda would be excited about him.

"And this guy was old?" he said.

"That's right!" Lucinda said. "That's the whole point! It means Mercedes Henderson isn't prejudiced against old people like Michael Strum."

"Michael Strum?" Ruben said.

"Never mind," Lucinda said. "Philip Harris was old. And Mercedes Henderson loved Philip Harris. And the characters in Kyle's dad's book are old. And Mercedes Henderson is feeling sentimental about old people right now. So there's even more of a chance she'll love Kyle's dad's characters. Which means she'll love Kyle's dad's book. Which means—"

"She'll publish Kyle's dad's book," Ruben said.

"Exactly," Lucinda said.

"So why is Kyle upset?"

"Because of the plan."

"I see."

"No, you don't see," Lucinda said. "I can tell by your eyes you don't see. But Kyle had a plan. And I skipped his plan. Or part of his plan. Because as soon as I left Saint Patrick's Cathedral I walked straight back to Boykin Books and took Kyle's dad's manuscript out of my backpack and wrote 'Attention: Mercedes Henderson' on the manila envelope and handed it to the security guard behind the marble desk. Which wasn't the plan. Or even close to the plan. But Kyle wasn't there. He didn't see Mercedes Henderson. He didn't hear all the things she had to say. So he doesn't know we don't need the plan. Not anymore. Because—"

But here Lucinda stopped.

Froze.

As a look of horror came over her face.

"What's wrong?" said Ruben.

"She'll never see it," said Lucinda.

"What?"

"She'll never see it!"

"What are you talking about?"

"I'm talking about Mercedes Henderson," said Lucinda. "She's a senior editor. Which, in the publishing world, means she's queen of the universe. If she isn't expecting a manuscript to arrive on her desk, she'll never even glance at it. No matter what it says on the envelope. No matter if her name is written in rhinestones!"

"So—," Ruben started.

"So I blew it!" Lucinda cut him off. "*Love in Autumn* will be just another book among the avalanche of all the other books that arrive at Boykin Books every single day. Never to be read. Certainly never to be published. Which was why Kyle knew he needed a plan. Which is why I ought to go find a great big hole in the ground, hop in, and fill it up with dirt."

Lucinda didn't, of course. Find a great big hole, I mean. But she did feel sorry for herself. And she did feel stupid. I mean, what was she thinking? How could she have been so illogical? None of which seemed to bother Ruben. Who was too busy staring at her dark brown eyes to worry about logic. Nor did it bother Mrs. Gomez. Who was still gripping the stairway railing, her fingers turning white every time Lucinda said the name *Mercedes Henderson*.

Chapter 17

Kyle knocked on Percy Percerville's door.

That's right. He didn't use his key. He didn't let himself in to wait for Shakespeare on the chair. He took hold of the polished silver knocker shaped like a sledgehammer, pulled it back, and let it fall onto the polished silver plate. The sound that followed was no simple *bong!* or *bang!* or *clang!* Nope. Not at Percy Percerville's house. Instead, it was Mozart's "Funeral March." Which, even if you don't recognize the name, you'd know the tune. Since it's played in movies and TV anytime there's danger or sadness or tragedy in the air:

Dum dum de-dum dum de-dum de-dum de-dum!

Kyle was ready for it. He'd heard it the first time he'd come to the house and knocked. And, yeah, it was creepy. Which may be why Kyle let the hammer fall. Because he'd had the creeps since he'd walked out his front door. Because Kyle had lived with his dad for lots and lots of years. Which meant Kyle knew what Lucinda had just figured out. That Mercedes Henderson would never look at his dad's manuscript. Not by handing it to the security guard. Which was why Kyle got the creeps when Lucinda told him she had. Which was why Kyle needed some new ideas. Which was why he pulled the hammer.

Whoooosh!

It wasn't that Percy flung the door open so quickly he created an air pocket that practically sucked Kyle right into the hallway that caused Kyle to chomp down on his tongue to keep from swallowing it. Nope. It was Percy Percerville himself. Or, at least, a *bald* Percy Percerville. That's right. Maybe Percy had been thrown off by the knock on a Friday afternoon. Or maybe he'd been so engrossed in another argument with his editor or one of Cynthia Marlow's famous topsy-turvy plot twists. Whatever, he forgot. His wig, I mean. And there he stood. Chin raised. Eyebrows squeezed into the bridge of his nose. Nostrils expanding and contracting like a bull at the sight of a matador's red cape.

"A key, my dear boy, a key!" he cried. "One of the wonders of mankind. A key will unlock a door. A key will unlock *this* door. A person may even want to try it sometime. You, for instance. Instead of disturbing the more industrious living occupants of a household at all hours of the afternoon."

"But—," Kyle started.

"No 'buts,'" Percy Percerville cut him off. "No 'excuse mes' or 'I'm sorrys' or 'it won't happen agains.' Because

I assure you, dear boy, it won't. It can't. It shan't. Do you know the pressure I'm under? The time constraints? The deadlines? No, of course you don't. But believe me, dear boy, they're considerable. Like a flame held under the balls of my feet. Like a vise squeezing the stem of my brain. Like a thumbscrew screwing my . . . well, I'm sure you can figure out what a thumbscrew screws. The point is, dear boy, I'm swamped. As in busy. As in too busy for anyone's 'but.' For you see, dear boy, I have plenty of 'buts' of my own. That's why I hired you. That's why you are under my employ. To take care of one of my 'buts'. One of my biggest 'buts.' Not add more 'buts' to my already 'but'-filled load. Am I making myself clear, dear boy? Have the 'but' interruptions been nipped in the bud, or shall I mention the unmentionables that shall occur to a certain someone the next time he knocks on doors and breaks the delicate balance of my already precarious . . ."

Who knows how long Percy Percerville's harangue might have lasted if, at that very moment, Shakespeare hadn't come tiptoeing into the hallway with you-know-what dangling from his mouth.

No, not another title page.

The wig.

Percy's wig.

Which didn't look quite as silly as you might expect. I mean, it looked silly. Or, at least, Shakespeare looked silly. With sort of a grayish, blueish, salt-and-pepper-ish hank of hair dangling down his chin like one of those beards the bad guys wear in cartoons, only you don't see a lot of bad-guy *dogs* in cartoons. But you know what I mean. Shakespeare looked silly. But the wig itself didn't look silly. It looked like a wig. Percy Percerville's wig. Enough so Percy Percerville figured out what it was in about half of a half of a half of a second.

But get this:

He didn't flip out.

What I mean is, he didn't scream. Or grab the top of his head. Or race over to Shakespeare and try to yank it out of his mouth. Or shout at Kyle to get out the door and never set foot in this house again. Or faint. Or cry. Or jump up and down. Or screech. Or even crack wise and say something to Shakespeare like: "No, dear boy. It certainly won't do. Never set foot downstairs in this household again until you've at least had a shave."

Nope.

None of that stuff.

He simply raised his eyebrows. And lowered his chin. As Shakespeare tiptoed over sideways and dropped the wig into Percy Percerville's outstretched hand. And still Percy didn't screech. Or blush. Or even attempt to mash the wig back on top of his slick, shiny scalp. Instead, he smiled. A first. Or at least it was the first time he'd ever smiled at Kyle.

"But?" Percy Percerville said.

Kyle said nothing.

"But?" Percy repeated.

Kyle was flabbergasted. The "But?" wasn't mean. It wasn't sarcastic. Percy said "But?" as if he wanted Kyle to finish the sentence.

"Why?" Kyle said.

"Why am I allowing you to state the purpose of your interruption now but not before?" Percy said.

Kyle nodded.

"Fair question," Percy said. "Deserves a fair answer." He raised his chin. He blinked. Once. Then he looked Kyle right in the eyes. "Because of your civilized response to my bald head."

He didn't say "hairless pate" or "dome à la mode" or "cranium sans toupee." Nothing fancy. Nothing cute. Which may have been why Kyle took the chance.

"I need help," he said.

Don't worry. Kyle wasn't about to break his promise. He wasn't going to threaten Percy with the Cynthia Marlow reward. But, at the same time, Kyle was determined to find out how a book got published. Not the inside stuff. Nothing that direct. Kyle couldn't risk it. But that was the trouble. I mean, how do you ask someone how to do something without coming right out and asking him how to do it?

Simple.

You lie.

"I want to be president," Kyle said.

"Of the United States, dear boy? Good luck."

"Of my high school class."

"Ah."

"Not this year. Next year."

"Hmm."

"But I want to plan it this year."

"Of course."

"A lot of people think it's silly to run for president," Kyle said. "Or, at least, a lot of people *say* it's silly. When most of them would be glad to be president. They just don't want to run. Because they don't want to lose. I mean, take a guy like me. It's, like, a one in a million shot I can win. But I don't care. I'm going to run anyway. And maybe I'll lose. But maybe not. Especially if I come up with a plan. A good plan. And not be afraid to make a fool of myself."

Percy cocked his eyebrows.

He crossed his arms.

The combination of these two, it seemed, caused Shakespeare to spring into action. He crossed the room backward. He pushed his rear end up so Percy would scratch him. Or pat him. Or both. Which Percy did. Which Shakespeare loved. So much so, Shakespeare closed his eyes and stretched his chin up as far as it would go and started jerking his back-right leg up and down like the crank shaft of a locomotive.

"A metaphor, dear boy," Percy said. "For the way most of us go about our lives."

Kyle looked puzzled.

So Percy ran it down for him:

"Running in place, dear boy. Motion without movement. Action without results. *Shakespeare* doesn't have a plan. *Shakespeare* won't become president of his high-school class. *You,* on the other hand—*you,* dear boy, just may. Why? Because while other lads your age are throwing round balls through hoops or kicking spherical objects through goal posts, you realize every worthwhile pursuit requires absolute precision with a dash of spontaneity."

"Excuse me?"

"A plan, dear boy. A plan."

"Oh."

"If you were extraordinarily handsome or a spectacular athlete, I'd say go with your strengths. But you have no strengths. No observable strengths. Or you wouldn't suffer my abuse so sheepishly."

"I guess not."

"Don't mope, dear boy. Your weakness *is* your strength. It allows you to use your wits. Which you've already proved you have in abundance by seeking my advice. You want to be president of your class, dear boy? Well, just remember this. It isn't what you *are* that matters. It's what people *think* you are."

Chapter 18

Eight P.M.

Four hours later.

Kyle, Chad, and Tyrone sat in the exact same seats in the exact same back booth at the Tofu Tutti-Frutti.

Lucinda?

Not there.

It wasn't that she refused to come. Kyle couldn't find her. Not by e-mail. Not by cell phone. Nothing. Zero. And, yeah, she might not like missing a meeting. But the secret agents had work to do. Tonight. Right now.

"Did you bring it?" said Kyle.

"How come *she's* not here?" said Chad.

"*She's* got a name," said Tyrone.

"Whatever," said Chad.

"Did you bring it?" said Kyle.

"Afraid to answer my question?" said Chad.

"Afraid to answer mine?" said Kyle.

"I brought it," said Chad.

"Hook it up," said Kyle.

It was a laptop. And you bet Chad brought it. He

brought it every place he could, anytime he could. Because he was one of the few kids he or anybody else knew who had one. And, of course, Chad rarely passed up an opportunity where he could show off.

"Hook it up where?" he said.

"Under the jukebox," Tyrone said.

Check it out:

Not only was the Tofu Tutti-Frutti so hip it served stuff no one really liked but ate anyway because it was like eating dessert that was supposed to be good for you, but every single one of the booths had free Internet docking stations. Kyle flashed to all the other coffee shops and soda fountains where no one was actually talking to anyone across the table but typing away in chat rooms to someone who may not even be living in the same country.

"I'm in," said Chad.

And he was.

"Yahoo" lit up across the screen. So did the ten thousand ads for movies and CDs and acne cream and Coca-Cola and Gap and Banana Republic and J. Crew and Lands' End. You know. You've seen them. Kyle certainly had. And was seeing them now. Though not really. They were all a blur. Like vegetable soup. Only more colorful.

"Type in 'literaryagents.com,'" he said.

"I thought we were the agents," said Chad.

"Just do it," said Kyle.

"Okay," said Chad.

"Okay," said Kyle.

And there it was:

How to Submit Your Manuscript.

Nothing fancy. Just a bunch of rules. Starting with "General" and ending with "Cover Letter" and all about as dry as dirt.

At least, as far as Chad was concerned.

"I thought secret agents were supposed to do cool stuff," he said. "Slip into disguises. Spy on the bad guys. Make out with babes. Not worry about double spacing on medium weight paper or using twelve-point fonts."

"You have to walk before you run," Tyrone said.

"Your mommy teach you that, Tofu Boy?" Chad said.

"You weren't talking so tough when Lucinda was here," Tyrone said.

"Well, then, she's lucky she's not here now," Chad said.

"Thanks for the warning," Lucinda said.

While Kyle was studying the computer screen and Chad was complaining and arguing with Tyrone, Lucinda had climbed the Tofu Tutti-Frutti's three front steps, pulled open the slick, stainless steel door, silently walked across the black-and-white-tiled floor, and arrived at the back booth just in time to hear how lucky she was.

And, oh yeah, there's one other thing:

She wasn't alone.

"Ruben?" said Tyrone.

"Tyrone," said Ruben.

Chad said nothing. Chad swallowed. Hard. Although most of what he swallowed was a lot of hot air.

In case you hadn't picked up on it, tension was mounting at the Tofu Tutti-Frutti. And I mean way beyond the usual bickering between Chad and Tyrone. The arrival of Lucinda moved it up a notch, sure. But the appearance of Ruben Gomez was like punching the accelerator to the floor. For starters, he was new to the group. But way, *way* beyond that, he was Ruben Gomez.

Think about it:

How many leaders can one group have?

One.

Period.

No exceptions.

And Kyle was the leader of the secret agents. Without question. But, now, here was Ruben. Who was always the leader. It didn't matter what group. Not that anyone ever voted. A vote was never necessary. Ruben won by acclamation. Silent acclamation. Every time.

So . . .

So you'd figure something had to give. Or, at least, that's what Chad and Tyrone figured. You could tell by the way their eyes kept darting back and forth between Kyle and Ruben. It would be hard to say, though, what Lucinda figured. Her eyes darted back and forth, all right. But their usual sparkle seemed less assured and more like a dare. Like she was waiting for Kyle to say something so she could pounce on it.

Only Kyle said nothing. He didn't even look up from the computer screen. It was almost as if he had expected Lucinda to show up with Ruben. And it wasn't that he was going out of his way to ignore them. Or that he was afraid. Or self-conscious. He truly seemed lost in concentration. As he scrolled the screen. Nodding every now and then. And smiling to himself. Or, at least, that was what he did most of the time. Because once, near the end, he stopped. And looked puzzled. And bit his lower lip. And squinted. Hard. Then scrolled the screen backward. Until his eyes locked on to what he was scrolling for. Which was when he nodded all over again. And smiled his secret smile. Only this time, he was no longer staring at the screen.

"It's not what you are. It's what people think you are," he said.

"Huh?" Chad said.

"Exactly," Kyle said. "It sounds like mumbo jumbo because it *is* mumbo jumbo. Until you add the second part."

"Which is?" Chad said.

"First, you have to have the goods," Kyle said.

"Am I the only moron on the planet?" Chad said. "Or would someone else like to know what Parker's blabbering about?"

And that wasn't all Chad didn't pick up on. Because, of course, he was too busy worrying about what he always worried about—himself. But Tyrone and Lucinda and Ruben caught Kyle's vibe big-time. The way his voice stayed quiet and never cracked. The way his fingers folded across one another and never twitched. The way his eyes locked on to their eyes and never blinked.

Who was in charge?

I'll let you figure that one out.

"Take basketball," Kyle said in that same steady voice. "When Ruben is in the game, the other team knows it. The other team *feels* it. You can see it in the players' faces. Ruben is the man. Ruben is clutch. Even *he* believes it. And it helps him. It gives him that extra step. Which makes him even better than he already is. But that's only part of it. The second part. Because here's the thing. Before he was the man, Ruben was still a great basketball player. He still had the goods."

"What's he talking about?" cried Chad. "Will someone please tell me what basketball has to do with getting a book published?"

Silence.

Tyrone didn't say anything because he was just about as lost as Chad, only he had the good sense to keep his mouth shut. Lucinda didn't say anything because, even though she thought she understood exactly what Kyle was talking about, she wasn't as sure of herself as she usually was because of the security guard fiasco. Kyle didn't say anything because . . . well . . . because he figured the whole thing was so obvious it didn't really need an explanation. Which left Ruben. Who surprised everyone. Especially himself. Not by his words. But by the way he said them. By his tone. Which pretty much told anyone who was paying attention that he wasn't trying to take over. He wasn't trying to be the boss. And, even more surprising, it was almost as if there were *relief* in his voice. As if he were almost thankful he could be in a group of kids his age and didn't *have* to take charge.

"Kyle's right," he said. "I can play ball. That's not bragging. Because there're plenty of guys who've got a better shot than I do. But I practice. I work at it. Hard. Harder than anybody around. And that's what gives me the edge."

"Ah!" said Chad. "So all Kyle's dad needs to do is work on his jump shot, and *Love in Autumn* is bound to be a best-seller!"

"Funny," said Lucinda.

"I knew there was a reason we didn't hang out," said Ruben.

"Only one?" said Tyrone.

But Kyle wasn't about to let this turn into a kick-Chad-while-he-was-being-a-jerk contest.

"My fault," Kyle said. "Blame me. I should have been more direct. I should have said *Love in Autumn* is a terrific book. Which is important. The *most* important. Because nothing else you do matters if you don't start there. But it's only the beginning. The next step is to make sure the book's in the right format. Which we're doing now. Which may sound dull. Which *is* dull. But I bet wind sprints aren't all that exciting either. But if Ruben didn't have the legs, he wouldn't hit the shot at the buzzer. Sorry. That was a slip. I'll lay off basketball and get back to books. Not all of them. Just my dad's."

He spun the screen around so the rest could see.

"There," he said. "Second sentence. Clear as day. 'If you break one of these rules, you could irritate an editor.' And I don't want to irritate an editor. I don't want to give anyone any reason *not* to publish this book. You with me?"

They all nodded.

"Chad?"

"I'm with you."

"Good. Let's go."

"Where?"

"Nowhere. I mean, read the rules."

"Why me?"

"Why not?"

And since Chad didn't have an answer (which may have been a first) he read. All sixteen pages. Out loud. In fact, he even got into it. Because it was easy. And everyone, including Lucinda, listened. Which made Chad the center of attention. Which, as you might imagine, he didn't exactly hate.

"We've got Times New Roman," said Kyle.

"Twelve-point font," said Tyrone.

"Unbound, medium-weight, letter-sized paper," said Lucinda.

"Headings?" said Chad.

"Check," said Ruben.

"Title page?"

"Check."

"Clear, clean photocopies?"

"Nah," said Kyle. "We'll print them off the disk."

"Cover letter?"

"Lucinda will write it," said Kyle.

"I will?" said Lucinda.

"You're the best writer," said Kyle.

"Is that so?" said Lucinda.

"And Chad just read that the cover letter is what the editor reads first," said Ruben.

"I can hear," said Lucinda.

"You'll do great," said Tyrone.

"I suppose I will," said Lucinda.

Who didn't blush when she said it. Not because she was bragging. But because she could feel it return. The confidence. Which, a few hours before, she wasn't sure she'd ever feel again. But here was Kyle. Trusting in her. Even after she messed up so badly. And Ruben.

The most famous kid who ever went to Roosevelt High practically turning into blubber every time she opened her mouth. Which was cool. Wonderful, even. But why didn't Kyle do that? Why did he barely look up from the computer screen? And worse—way worse—why did she care?

"That it?" Ruben said.

"That's it," Kyle said.

"What's it?" Chad said.

"We've got the goods," Kyle said. "Except . . ."

"Except what?" Tyrone said.

"My father's name," Kyle said. "Walter. We're going to stop calling my father Walter."

"I never call your father Walter," Chad said.

"What's wrong with Walter?" Tyrone said.

"It's got no mystery," Kyle said.

"Huh?" Chad said.

"How about his initials?" Lucinda said.

"W. J. Parker?" Kyle said.

"Not bad," Tyrone said.

"Not bad at all," Ruben said.

And, for the first time in three days, Kyle smiled.

Chapter 19

You haven't met Alexa Blake yet.

But she was old.

Sixty-three years old. And always wore a dress—never a skirt, certainly never slacks—and pulled her hair back in a bun so tight she practically yanked the strands out by the roots. Which, as you might imagine, made her appear severe. So much so, that the following Monday Chad would have definitely felt a shiver shoot up his spine if he saw her raise one of her razor-thin eyebrows. Which she did quite frequently. Which she was doing now. At Chad. Though Chad wasn't aware of it. Since Alexa Blake was raising that eyebrow while she spoke to Chad over the phone.

"W. J. Parker must cancel his luncheon appointment tomorrow with Mr. Boykin? Who is W. J. Parker? Are you sure you have the right Mr. Boykin? *Harry R.* Boykin? President and publisher of Boykin Books?"

Why Chad?

Why was he making the call?

Because this was it. His moment. The moment Kyle always knew would come. When the secret agents would need that voice. Chad's voice. The voice he used to describe what his scalpel would be doing to his classmates in the not-so-distant future. You see, Tyrone could sing. And Ruben could hit a jump shot. And Lucinda could come up with more facts than all the rest of the secret agents put together. But no one—I mean *no one*—could make your teeth clench and your fingers ball into a fist faster than Chad Simon's nasal sneer. One syllable and you wanted to scream. Or kick your dog. Or punch *yourself* in the stomach.

Oh, sure, there'd been a tryout. Over the weekend, Kyle had all the secret agents hold a receiver up to their mouths and talk in their meanest, nastiest, I'm-smarter-than-you'll-ever-be tones of voice. But it really wasn't much of a contest. I mean, Lucinda was the clear runner-up when she pretended she was Percy Percerville and said: "No, dear boy. I simply wouldn't dream of drinking a cup of tea wearing argyle socks!" But even Tyrone had to admit the whole thing was a done deal the moment Chad cleared his throat.

"Of course I have the right Mr. Boykin!" Chad snapped into the mouthpiece as he raised an eyebrow of his own. "Just tell him W. J. Parker must cancel his appointment. Better yet, write it down."

"Who do you think you're talking to, Mr.—"

"Simon!" Chad cut her off. "As in Simon Says! And I say I'm talking to Alexa Blake, Mr. Boykin's personal assistant."

"If you know who I am, Mr. *Simon* Says, then you know I make all of Mr. Boykin's appointments. And, I must tell you, I have no record of a W. J. Parker. I've never heard of him. And even if I had, I would never have made a luncheon appointment for Mr. Boykin tomorrow since Mr. Boykin is vacationing in Palma, Spain."

"All the more reason for you to write it down! Oh, and Miss Blake? No need to concern yourself. Your slipup is safe with me."

"*My* slipup?"

"Well, it certainly wasn't W. J. Parker who made the luncheon appointment while Mr. Boykin was out of the country."

"Who is this W. J. Parker?"

"He's not a *this*!" cried Chad. "He's a *Mr.*! And really, Miss Blake, I don't believe it's my place to tell you what your boss so obviously is trying to keep to himself!"

Click!

Chad pushed the End button.

The line went dead.

Which should have led to some backslapping and high fives echoing off Kyle's living-room walls—Kyle's *clean* living-room walls. After all, Chad not only followed Kyle's script but also added a few flourishes of his own that couldn't help but cause Alexa Blake to get so hopping mad she'd make it her business to find out exactly who this W. J. Parker was. Which she couldn't do without spreading his name around. Which, of course, was the whole point of the phone call.

Let's face it, though. The same skills that sent Alexa Blake into a rage were equally effective now. Or, put another way, Chad wasn't a high five kind of a guy. Don't get me wrong. The phone call was a success. The gang was wired. *Kyle* was wired. But the way Chad flicked his eyebrows after clicking off, then tossed the phone into Lucinda's lap as if to say, "Beat that, girlie," pretty much muffled any outward signs of Kyle's secret agent society melding into a single fighting unit. Which wasn't all bad. Not the no-melding part. That certainly wasn't so hot. It's the no-celebrating part I'm talking about. Or, at least, what Kyle would have been talking about had he been talking about it. Because he knew the phone call was just their first move. And he was already planning their second.

"We need a woman," he said.

"Excuse me?" Lucinda said.

"Calm down. I meant someone older than us."

"How old?" Ruben said.

"Doesn't matter," Kyle said. "As long as she's old enough to go to one of those hair salon places."

"Like me?" said Mrs. Gomez.

That's right.

She'd been hiding on the stairs again and practically leaped over the railing the moment Kyle mentioned the secret agents needed a woman.

"Huh?" Ruben said.

Which wasn't like him at all. I mean, Ruben didn't usually say lame-o things like "Huh?" But let's face it. Anyone can get shook up. And Ruben was. Big-time. Because, first off, it was obvious his grandmother had been spying on them. And, second off, she was wearing her uniform. And this time it wasn't just in front of Kyle. This time it was also in front of Chad and Tyrone and (worst of all) Lucinda.

Chad and Tyrone?

They were shook up, sure. But not because Mrs. Gomez was spying on them and certainly not because she was wearing a maid's uniform. They were shook up because an adult had overheard Chad make a prank phone call, and both were now certain they'd be grounded for the rest of their lives or (in Tyrone's case) forced to eat bean curd until he was twenty-one.

Lucinda?

She was shook up too. But not because of Mrs. Gomez. Or not directly because of Mrs. Gomez. Lucinda was shook up because Kyle was shook up because Mrs. Gomez could bust the secret agent society to his mom or, worse, Alexa Blake.

In other words, everyone was shook up. Including Mrs. Gomez. Whose heart was beating against her ribs like an xylophone. Though she wasn't about to show it. I mean, these were just kids. And one of them was her grandson. And she'd been waiting for an opportunity like this for so long she wasn't about to blow it before she even got started.

"I go to a hair salon once a week," she said.

"Really?" said Kyle.

"Really," said Mrs. Gomez.

Which was weird.

Way weird.

Because that was the exact word Mercedes Henderson was saying at that exact moment. No, she wasn't in Kyle's living room saying "Really" to the secret agents plus Mrs. Gomez. Mercedes Henderson was across town in her corner office in the Boykin Books Building on the fifty-sixth floor. You'd think the most famous editor alive would be poring over the galleys of her next new smash or deep in movie residual negotiations with Paramount Pictures. But no. She was tapping her right pointer finger on her glass-topped desk. She was rubbing her left palm across her black mesh chair. She was staring straight at the stiletto eyebrow of Alexa Blake.

"Really," said Mercedes Henderson.

"W. J. Parker," said Alexa Blake. "You sure you haven't heard of him?"

"Positive."

"And you didn't set up a luncheon appointment for him with Mr. Boykin?"

"That might be a bit difficult since I've never heard of W. J. Parker."

"It wouldn't be the first time," said Alexa Blake.

"That I set up an appointment with Mr. Boykin for someone I'd never heard of?"

"That you set up an appointment with Mr. Boykin behind my back."

"Gee," said Mercedes Henderson, "I'm really enjoying this conversation."

She was being sarcastic, of course. Mercedes Henderson wasn't enjoying this conversation in the least. Here she was, the editor with more hits on her hands than all the other editors in the building put together, being scolded like a first grader by someone *People* magazine and *The New York Times Book Review* had never even heard of. But since Mr. Boykin would rather lose his right arm than lose Alexa Blake, there wasn't much Mercedes Henderson could do about it. Except quit. Which she wasn't about to do. Not when there was a new writer out there who must be so good Mr. Boykin was keeping him a secret even from the woman he trusted more than anyone else in the world.

"What did you say Mr. Parker's initials were again?" said Mercedes Henderson.

"Very funny," said Alexa Blake.

And she grabbed the bun in the back of her head and gave her already yanked hair another stiff yank. Which, I suppose, was meant to scare Mercedes Henderson. But all it did was provide Alexa Blake with such a searing, screeching headache that it instantaneously brought tears to her eyes. Which left her two options. She could stand there and cry in front of Mercedes Henderson. Or she could stomp out. Which was a no-brainer. She stomped out. Giving Mercedes Henderson the opportunity to grab her Kate Spade purse by its two-toned leather strap, unsnap the solid gold clasp, flip open her alligator notepad, and print:

Parker, W. J.

Mercedes Henderson was wrong about one thing, however. *People* magazine had heard about Alexa Blake. Or at least, someone on the staff had. Since three years before, in a four-page cover story where Harry Boykin was called "the playboy polo player who also happens to own Boykin Books," Alexa Blake was mentioned once— paragraph 27, line 3:

In matters of business, however, Harry Boykin never makes a move without first consulting his longtime personal assistant, Alexa Blake.

But once was enough.

As far as Kyle was concerned, that is. After six hours on the Internet, he'd come to agree with Lucinda that Mercedes Henderson was not only the most likely editor to publish *Love in Autumn* but also the best. But he didn't stop there. He scrolled through Boykin Books' list of authors, best-sellers, number of submissions through agents in the past five years, ratio of rejections to acceptances, and eighteen articles on Harry Boykin. Which was where he ran across the name Alexa Blake. Which was where he came up with the idea:

Mystery.

Intrigue.

That's what Percy Percerville meant when he said, "It's not what you are. It's what people think you are."

Or, in this case, "It's what people think your *book* is."

If Harry Boykin didn't make a professional move without first consulting Alexa Blake, then Alexa Blake might get upset if, suddenly, he had. *Any* move. Even a date for lunch. A made-up date, sure. But Alexa Blake wouldn't know that. Not if Harry Boykin wasn't around to set her straight.

And why wouldn't he be around?

Because every article Kyle read mentioned that Harry Boykin always spent the first three weeks of June in Palma, Spain. Without a phone. Without a fax machine. *Incommunicado.* His way to unwind. Catch his breath. Disassociate himself from the life that was Harry Boykin. In other words, he was unavailable. No one could reach him. No one could find out if he had, in fact, set up a lunch date with W. J. Parker. Not even his personal assistant. Especially his personal assistant. Who wouldn't like it if he had. Who might even get mad. Really mad. Mad enough to check it out. Spread the name around the office. No, not Harry Boykin—*W. J. Parker.*

Of course, Kyle never dreamed Alexa Blake would walk right into Mercedes Henderson's office and announce W. J. Parker less than two minutes after the phone call. He had no way of knowing about the feud that had been raging between them for the past six years. He hoped a rumor would start. Slow at first. Then build momentum. Maybe it would take a day. Maybe a week. But Kyle was hoping that some way, somehow, someone at Boykin Books would whisper or say or scream the name *W. J. Parker* to Mercedes Henderson.

Not that he was counting on it. He had other tricks up his sleeves. But again, as luck would have it, he had no idea Mrs. Gomez would step into his living room and volunteer.

"One condition," she said.

"Yeah?" Kyle said.

"I'm writing a book," Mrs. Gomez said.

"You're what?" Ruben said.

"I'm writing a book," Mrs. Gomez repeated. "And when I finish, I want Kyle to help me publish it."

Have you ever had anyone believe in you? I don't mean hope for the best or wish you luck. I mean put her faith in you. Look at you as if you're the one—maybe the only one—who could make her wish come true. Sure, Kyle's dad gave him a wink every time he stepped to the plate, and his mom always said, "Nothing to worry about, dear. You'll ace the math test!" I'm not talking about your parents. They *have* to believe in you. It's kind of like believing in themselves. I'm talking about someone else. Someone not connected with you. Even if she's someone else's grandma.

"But—," Ruben started.

"But nothing, sonny boy!" Mrs. Gomez snapped. "I just bought *The Thank You Book for Kids*. And you know who the author is? A fourteen-year-old girl named Ali. That's right. Fourteen years old! You know what that tells me? No one is too young or too old to do something she sets her mind on doing. That's what it tells me. You think because I scrub and sweep all day I can't write a book? Well, Mr. Ruben Gomez, you've got another think coming. I've even come up with a title for it—*Any Idiot Can Clean a House*. That's why I've been taking notes for the past six months. And you know something? They're funny. Every time I jot one down, I laugh. Out loud! Can you imagine an old lady laughing like a lunatic over scrubbing a floor? Well, I can. Because I do. Though that's probably as far as I ever would have taken it. Until I listened to you guys talking. Until I listened to *Kyle* talking. Because that's when I heard it. Loud and clear. The determination in his voice. And right away I knew he was going to do it. I knew he was going to get his dad's book published. I didn't know how. I wasn't even sure if he knew how. But I knew he was going to do it. And if he could do it for his dad, why not me?"

"Why not?" said Kyle.

"Huh?" said Ruben.

"Do we have a deal?" said Mrs. Gomez.

"Sure," said Kyle. "Right after we—"

"Get Mercedes Henderson to say yes to *Love in Autumn,*" Mrs. Gomez cut Kyle off.

Chapter 20

Frederico.

No. Excuse me. Not Frederico. *Mr.* Frederico. That was the adopted name of Frederick Patrick Harrison. Never mind he was born and raised in Oxford, Mississippi, thirty-three years before and had never so much as stuck his big toe on Italian soil. Call him Frederick or Fred and you may end up with a shaved head and a streak of orange dissecting your scalp. Because that was his business. Hair, I mean. Though you would never have been able to tell it from the sign on his salon door:

MR. FREDERICO'S

That was it.

Not MR. FREDERICO'S HAIRCUTTERS or MR. FREDERICO'S HAIRSTYLISTS. Just MR. FREDERICO'S. Period. If you didn't know what happened inside MR. FREDERICO'S on Madison Avenue between Sixty-first and Sixty-second Streets, Mr. Frederico didn't want you to know. Because it meant you were one of *them*—the *non*rich, *non*beautiful, *non*-famous, *non*–New Yorkers.

Oh, sure, you were probably all right in your way. It just wasn't Mr. Frederico's way. Which meant spending more money on a trim and blow dry than most people spend on food for their family for a week. All for the privilege of sitting in the cramped, crowded, way-too-hip waiting area on one of the chrome-and-leather chairs especially designed to twist your spine into a pretzel for over an hour until summoned into the presence of the great man himself, where you would be summarily scolded for failing to properly exercise your follicles. Mr. Frederico's word for *hair*. Mr. Frederico never said "hair." Wasn't saying it now, in fact. Wednesday. Two days after Mrs. Gomez made the appointment. Which was fortunate. The appointment, I mean. Since usually you had to wait a lot longer than two days.

"Ms. Gomez?" said the woman behind the chrome-and-glass counter with the name BLAZE stitched across the front of her T-shirt. "Mr. Frederico will be with you as soon as he finishes shouting at you-know-who."

And Mrs. Gomez did know. Everybody in the United States knew. Because, at that moment, Mr. Frederico just happened to be shouting at the highest-paid actress in Hollywood history. And, no, I can't tell you her name. But I can tell you that her one and only response to this abuse was to smile her famous smile at this pudgy man

157

with the ponytail who was wagging a highly buffed fingernail an inch in front of her face. Because that was another thing about Mr. Frederico's. Every famous woman living in Manhattan or visiting Manhattan or traveling within a fifty-mile radius of Manhattan made an appointment, waited patiently on one of the torture chairs, and got shouted at equally. No exceptions. No special favors for the rich or powerful. Everyone waited. Everyone had the fingernail wagged in her face. All for under four hundred dollars. If she was lucky.

"You smile?" shrieked Mr. Frederico. "You mock Mr. Frederico? You do not take Mr. Frederico seriously?"

"I'm so sorry!"

"Humph!"

"I'll try to do better!"

"*Try?* You say '*try*' to Mr. Frederico? Well, *try* taking that cobweb of yours to the nearest spider! Let him *try* to catch flies with it!"

"No! I mean, yes! I mean, I will! Do better! I promise!"

Mr. Frederico crossed his arms. He raised his chin. He pursed his lips. He tapped his silver snakeskin boot. He uncrossed his arms. He ran his index finger over his pierced right ear. He stopped. He froze. He seemed to have reached some sort of decision. Because suddenly, without warning, he tossed his hand over his head and began snapping his fingers as if he were trying to catch the attention of a not-so-intelligent poodle.

"Blaze! Blaze! Blaze!" he shouted. "Escort Ms. Movie Star to the body-and-sheen tub and submerge her scalp for at least forty-five minutes before they bring back *The Wizard of Oz* and force her to play the scarecrow."

"As you wish," Blaze said.

"As you wish, *Mr. Frederico,*" Mr. Frederico said.

"As you wish, *Mr. Frederico,*" Blaze repeated.

Blaze, as I'm sure you've figured out for yourself, was the woman behind the chrome-and-glass counter with the name BLAZE stitched across her T-shirt. Blaze was in her mid-twenties (of course) and thin (of course) and wore black (of course) and a barbed wire tattoo on her left upper arm (of course) and had the thickest, straightest, longest, most spectacular hair in midtown Manhattan (of course), but that was where the stereotype ended. Because, unlike Mr. Frederico, Blaze was neither snappy nor snippy. She played the good cop to Mr. Frederico's bad. They were kind of like a tag team match. Or a cat fight. He scratched. She purred. All part of the show. A show, by the way, that Mercedes Henderson had seen many times before.

Yeah, yeah. I know. That's really a cheat. I should have already mentioned that Mercedes Henderson was seated in the way-too-hip waiting area close enough to Mrs. Gomez that the two of them could have rubbed noses. But I knew you knew Mercedes Henderson was there. Of course she was there. Why else would Kyle have put the spinal column of Ruben Gomez's grandmother in such jeopardy?

And just for the record:

Mercedes Henderson hadn't uttered a peep. Not one. All she'd done since she first pushed open the chrome-and-glass door (with the name MR. FREDERICO'S etched into the glass) and crossed the white terrazzo floor (with the name MR. FREDERICO'S chiseled into the terrazzo) was park herself on one of those lovely chrome-and-leather chairs and hide her face inside a back issue of *Vogue* (with the name MR. FREDERICO'S scrawled across the plastic cover). It wasn't as if she'd been chatting nonstop on her cell phone or sharing split-end secrets with Blaze. I mean, no one inside Mr. Frederico's who hadn't already seen or known or read about Mercedes Henderson could have told you what color her eyes were, because she hadn't even taken off her sunglasses. And she might never have. If Mrs. Gomez hadn't gotten in her face:

"So you're the one," said Mrs. Gomez.

"Excuse me?" said Mercedes Henderson.

"I guess you should excuse yourself," said Mrs. Gomez.

"Excuse me?" repeated Mercedes Henderson.

"No need to overdo it," said Mrs. Gomez. "Once was sufficient."

Which was when Mercedes Henderson took off her sunglasses. And focused on Mrs. Gomez. Who, as you might imagine, was focusing right back.

"Do I know you?" said Mercedes Henderson.

"No," said Mrs. Gomez. "But I know you. Editor of *I'm Yours* and *He Won My Heart*. And, yes, they were fine books. Excellent books. But . . ."

"But?" said Mercedes Henderson.

"But they were about young people," said Mrs. Gomez.

"So?" said Mercedes Henderson.

"So all the books you edit are about young people," said Mrs. Gomez.

"Your point?" said Mercedes Henderson.

"You're a bright, young woman," said Mrs. Gomez. "I'm betting you'll figure that one out by yourself."

As you might imagine, this conversation was not going unnoticed by the other women, with too much time and too much money, crammed into Mr. Frederico's waiting area. Indeed, it wasn't going unnoticed by the man with the ponytail himself. You see, it had been a while—a very *long* while—since anyone other than Mr. Frederico had commanded this much attention at Mr. Frederico's. In other words, he wasn't used to sharing the spotlight. In other words, those snakeskin boots weren't exactly kicking up their heels with glee.

"Next!" Mr. Frederico snapped.

Mrs. Gomez didn't move.

"Must I repeat myself?" Mr. Frederico hissed. "I said 'next'!"

This time Mrs. Gomez did move. Not that she got up. Not even close. Instead, she turned. Or, at least, her neck did. Just enough to stare. Straight into Mr. Frederico's aqua-tinted contact lenses.

And yawn.

Yeah, you heard me.

She yawned. Nothing subtle, either. I mean, she arched her back and stretched her arms and half sighed, half moaned so loud she rattled the floor-to-ceiling mirrored display case of Mr. Frederico's Follicle Fresheners.

So okay. So what was happening at this particular moment in this particular hair salon may not have had the same historical significance as desegregating the South or landing an astronaut on the moon. But no one—I mean *no one*—had ever *not* leaped out of her chair the moment Mr. Frederico snapped, "Next!" It was like spitting in church. Like not offering your seat to a pregnant woman. Like refusing to curtsy when you met the queen of England.

Picture the scene:

Mr. Frederico. Scissors and styling comb stuck in his silver-studded belt, six-gun style, staring daggers through the hearts of all the women brave or stupid enough to stare back. And, believe me, there were plenty of women staring. Twelve, counting Blaze. All waiting for the six or seven zillion framed photographs of celebrities to start falling off Mr. Frederico's walls. Or for the floor to crack open. Or for the planets to collide. Or for something equally catastrophic to happen to the woman who didn't hop to when Mr. Frederico said hop to.

"Oh, get over yourself," said Mrs. Gomez.

"Are you talking to me?" said Mr. Frederico.

"Yes, Frederico. I'm talking to you."

"Did you call me 'Frederico'?"

"You know who you remind me of?" said Mrs. Gomez, pushing herself out of her chair and strolling in Mr. Frederico's direction. "My grandson. He's nicer than you, of course. But he equates dribbling a basketball with being a genius. You cut hair, Frederico. It grows on people's heads, and you cut it. Sometimes you wash it. Sometimes you dye it different colors. But most of the time you cut it. When you do a bad job, the hair grows back. When you do a good job, guess what, Frederico? The hair *still* grows back. And then you have to cut it all over again. I'm not saying it's not important for people to look good. I'm not saying it isn't nice if you can keep your more famous clientele off the 'Ten Worst Haircuts' list. But that doesn't make you a tortured soul, Frederico. No one would ever accuse you of suffering for your art. You know what you are, Frederico? You're a silly little man wearing silly little boots, who wouldn't know a genius if W. J. Parker himself walked in here, purchased a bottle of your phoney-baloney body-and-sheen cream, and squeezed it right up your nose."

"Did you say W. J. Parker?" Mercedes Henderson cried.

"Yes, I did, dear," Mrs. Gomez said.

And walked out the door.

Chapter 21

Okay. All right. The setup was complete. Mercedes Henderson was primed. Wired. Ready as she would ever be to read *Love in Autumn* by W. J. Parker. All Kyle had to do was get his dad's manuscript into her hands.

That was all.

Nothing more.

No sweat.

All he had to do was walk into her office. *After* he got off the elevator. *After* he walked past the guard.

Ah!

The guard!

The Boykin Books security guard!

With the marble jaw!

And no-nonsense eyes!

Which Lucinda had told Kyle about.

All about.

Which was why Kyle was up in his room later that night surfing the Net. For a clue. Something. Anything. To make it past that guard. Which turned out to be less like surfing and more like a really long ocean voyage. I mean, yeah, he stopped for supper. And for the thirty-five minutes it took to fake out his mom that he'd gone to sleep. But that was it. For the rest of the evening and half the night, Kyle sat bathed in that blue-green glow of his PC screen. Punching the keys. Clicking the mouse. Yawning. Stretching. Slapping himself silly trying to keep himself awake.

Mercedes Henderson didn't help. I mean, the articles about her in *People* and *Newsweek* and the *New York Times* and every other magazine and newspaper Kyle read and reread didn't help. Well, one did. Sort of. A *Newsweek* article six months back told Kyle that Mercedes Henderson left her office every day at 6 P.M. to work out with her personal trainer. Which meant Kyle could sneak *Love in Autumn* onto her desk *after* 6 P.M. Which was something. Something good. Something helpful. But there wasn't anything anywhere that gave Kyle even a hint how to slip past that guard. Which meant Kyle had to think outside the box. He had to come up with something that had nothing to do with Mercedes Henderson. Which wasn't easy. Not with his eyelids drooping. And his stomach rumbling because he hadn't eaten for nearly five hours.

Bong!

One A.M.

Bong! Bong!

Two A.M.

Bong! Bong! Bong!

The grandfather clock in the downstairs hall struck the hour again, but this time Kyle didn't hear it. He wouldn't have heard a bomb exploding unless someone dropped it right on his keyboard. No, he hadn't passed out. Nor was he daydreaming. But he was gone, all right. Long gone. Gone inside a pop-up ad for Giovanni's Pizza.

Maybe it was because he was hungry.

Or dead tired.

Or both.

Whatever, he suddenly saw it. Like one of those visions people seen in the desert. Only this one wasn't a mirage. This one was real. Kyle knew. He was sure of it.

How?

Because everyone eats pizza!

Five seconds later Kyle was tiptoeing down the stairs. Then pushing open his front door. Then racing across the street. Then throwing a pebble at Lucinda's window. Then another. Then another. Until the light in her room flipped on. And she stuck her face against the screen. But had to blink once or twice before she finally focused on Kyle with her sleepy eyes.

"What time is it?" she called down.

"Pizza!" Kyle called back.

"Huh?" Lucinda said.

"That's how we'll make it past the guard!" Kyle said.

"Pizza?" Lucinda said.

"Think about it!" Kyle said.

So Lucinda did. Since she had time. I mean, of course she had time. It was 3:30 A.M. Plus, there was all day at school. And the forty-five minutes it would take for Kyle and Shakespeare to go for their walk. So Lucinda had over thirteen hours to figure out what Kyle was going to do with a pizza.

Smash it into the guard's face?

Cut out the eyes and nose and wear it as a mask?

Nor was that all Kyle asked Lucinda to think about. There was also the note. The one he asked her to write before he raced back across the street and disappeared inside his front door. So Lucinda did. She wrote the note the next morning. During recess. Not on the computer. She wrote it by hand. On a Post-it. And, just as Kyle had instructed, she didn't put a name on it. She left it unsigned.

"Perfect!" Kyle shouted.

"What?" Lucinda shouted back.

"The note!" Kyle shouted. "It's perfect!"

"Oh!" Lucinda shouted back.

They were shouting because they were riding on the E train. The same subway Lucinda had taken to Fifty-third Street last Friday. Only this time Kyle had a plan. Only Kyle still hadn't told Lucinda the plan. Not all of it. Which Lucinda didn't get. Which Kyle didn't get either. Why he wasn't telling her, I mean. He was nervous. He knew that. He could have told her that. Though he didn't want to. Since he wanted to play it cool. Like he had ice water in his veins. Like Ruben. Who even in double overtime acted about as shook up as someone sipping lemonade under an umbrella at the beach.

Ruben.

Ruben liked Lucinda. Kyle could tell. Anyone could. All you had to do was check out the way the pupils in Ruben's eyes sparkled like stars on a mountain lake every time Lucinda even breathed.

So?

So why did Kyle care?

Since we're only talking about Ruben Gomez here. Since what girl was going to pick a guy like Ruben over a guy like Kyle? Every single one of them, that's who. I mean, let's face it. Kyle in double overtime? Gasping for breath. Tripping over his own feet. Dribbling the ball off his big toe.

Kind of like now.

I mean, give me a break. I mean, Kyle was so shook up, he had to pretend he wasn't by telling himself he'd figured something out Lucinda hadn't. Which, ridiculously enough, made him even more shook up. Since he also told himself that if Lucinda hadn't figured it out, maybe it wasn't such a hot idea after all.

"Almost there!" Kyle shouted.

"Where?" Lucinda shouted back.

But Kyle didn't answer. Not right away. First he shrugged. Then he blinked. Then he sucked that subway air deep into his lungs. Or he tried to. Since the air barely made it past his esophagus. Was it because it was 5:30? Which meant it was rush hour? Which meant it was about as hot and crowded as the subway gets? Was that the reason Kyle was having trouble breathing? And his ears were ringing? And the sweat was dripping down his neck? And his feet were going numb? And the left side of his face was beginning to twitch? And Lucinda's face was going in and out of focus?

I don't think so.

And neither did Kyle.

"The pizza!" he finally shouted.

"Yeah?" Lucinda shouted.

"I'm going to pretend I'm a pizza delivery boy!"

"You're going to deliver a pizza to Mercedes Henderson?"

"No!" Kyle shouted. "I'm going to ditch the pizza as soon as I make it past the guard!"

Lucinda didn't answer. She didn't have time. Kyle finished that last sentence just as the subway brakes started to shriek, and the E train pulled to a stop on Fifty-third Street. Which meant Lucinda and Kyle were pushed along by the crowd getting off and had to zigzag their way along the platform and up the stairs. The sidewalk was nearly as crowded as the subway. Lucinda grabbed Kyle's hand, and, once again, the two of them were swept along by the crush of people. Though not for long. Because right on the corner of Fifty-third Street and Fifth Avenue (ten steps from the subway stairs) was Giovanni's Pizzeria.

Coincidence?

It would have been.

If Kyle hadn't checked out the address on the pop-up ad.

"A medium cheese to go," Kyle said.

The guy behind the counter, with the apron smeared with marinara sauce, didn't answer. Nor did he look up from chopping the onions on his butcher block. Nor did he stop chopping the onions. Nor did he shrug. Nor shake his head. Nor perform any other type of body language that would have informed Kyle that he (the guy behind the counter) was aware of Kyle's existence. Someone who wasn't from New York would probably have figured the guy hadn't heard Kyle. Which, of course, wasn't the case at all. It was just that the guy behind the counter was acting like a guy behind a counter. Or, at least, he was acting like a New York guy behind a New York pizzeria counter.

In other words, he'd make the pizza. In his own time. At his own pace. And there'd be no "Coming right up" or "It's a hot one out there" or any other kind of chitchat that might make his day and yours any more pleasant.

Which was just what Lucinda had been waiting for. The silence, I mean. She hadn't been able to say anything to Kyle since he told her about his delivery boy scheme. A scheme she liked, by the way. Thought was brilliant even. So brilliant she couldn't figure out why she hadn't thought of it herself. Though she didn't say that. Instead, she said:

"I wish I was the one delivering the pizza."

"Me too."

"What?"

"I've never done anything like this. I don't know how I'll act."

"No one knows how he's going to act until he acts."

"What's that supposed to mean?"

"Kyle," said Lucinda. "All primates are programmed with the fight or flight response. Our pupils dilate. Our pulses palpitate. Our palms perspire."

"You're showing off again," said Kyle.

"All I'm saying," said Lucinda, "is that these are the times we know we're the most alive."

"Oh, I'm alive, all right," said Kyle.

He didn't see her smile at this last sentence. He was too busy seeing himself blow it. You know, tripping. Or getting tongue-tied. Or just plain fainting right there in front of the guard. Yep. Lucinda was right. She should have been going in instead of him. Except the guard had already seen her. And, anyway, it wasn't her dad's book. So if anyone was going to submit *Love in Autumn* it was going to be Kyle.

If submit was the right word.

Since it was more like breaking and entering.

Or fraud.

Or both.

The pizza cost $12.95. And, yeah, that was a lot of money. But Kyle didn't mind. He would have paid four times that much if he could have come up with a different way to do what he was about to do.

"Okay," said Lucinda.

"Okay, what?" said Kyle.

"I'll be right here," said Lucinda.

She meant in the park. The pocket park with the chunk of the Berlin Wall straight across the street from the Boykin Books breezeway. That was the plan. She was supposed to keep a lookout. And call Kyle as soon as Mercedes Henderson left the building.

"Your cell phone's on Vibrate, right?" said Lucinda.

"Right."

"That's it, then."

This time Kyle didn't say, "What's it?" He didn't play dumb. Or cute. Because he didn't feel like either. Because it was time. For the real part. Or the scary part. Or whatever you call it when your heart starts hammering and your mouth goes dry. Because across the street and down the breezeway and through the revolving glass door was the gray marble sculpture of the book and the gray marble floor and the gray marble desk and walls and casing around the elevators and, of course, the guard. Who wasn't gray marble. But may as well have been.

Kyle felt himself take a deep breath. He didn't tell himself to. It wasn't a conscious thing. He just breathed in automatically. The same way he shrugged his shoulders to adjust the weight of his backpack and tried to stop his hand from shaking under the pizza box. It didn't work, of course. Kyle couldn't stop his hand from shaking anymore than he could stop his teeth from clicking like castanets or his heart from pounding like a tom-tom. Though he didn't slow down. Not once. Not even for a second. He just took one last deep breath and pushed the Boykin Books Building's revolving glass door.

And saw him.

In that gray uniform.

With that marble jaw.

Was it Kyle's imagination? Or had those slate blue eyes suddenly gone narrow? Were the guard's thumb and forefinger all set to unsnap his walkie-talkie and put out an SOS to all his security-guard buddies within a half mile of the Boykin Books doorstep?

Nope.

Not even close.

Instead, he winked.

That's right.

Winked.

As soon as he caught a glimpse of the pizza box.

"Okay, kid," the guard said as if he and Kyle were long-lost pals. "Get on up there and pronto."

Are you kidding me?

I mean, sure, Kyle was nervous. And his mind was racing faster than Shakespeare's back leg when you scratched his rump. But Kyle was ready for this. He was all set to tell the guard that Mercedes Henderson had called out for a medium cheese to be delivered to one of her assistants who had to work late on a manuscript. In other words, Kyle was ready to tell a bald-faced lie. With his knees and ankles and every other joint in his body turning to butter. And his throat squeezing itself shut. All for nothing. For the guard to wink. And smile. And shoo Kyle right through.

Almost.

"Hey!" the guard suddenly cried.

Kyle froze.

"You're new, aren't you?"

Kyle nodded.

"Have a good flight," the guard said.

Which was supposed to be a joke. Which Kyle could tell. Not only because the guard winked again but also because his jaw stopped looking like marble and started looking more like Silly Putty. So Kyle smiled. Even though he didn't get it. Not then. Not until the elevator doors closed and Kyle punched the button to floor fifty-six and suddenly felt as if he'd been beamed aboard the starship *Enterprise*. His heart dropped into his belly. His brain dropped into his feet. And, just for good measure, his Adam's apple started hopping up and down like a pogo stick.

Because Kyle was gulping.

Or trying to.

Because part of Kyle never believed he'd make it past the guard. Because, let's face it, someone must have tried the pizza trick before. I mean, it wasn't all that clever. At least, that was the way Kyle saw it. Except Kyle saw it wrong. No one had. Or, at least, no one told the guard. Because there he was. Kyle, I mean. Inside the elevator. Shooting toward the fifty-sixth floor as if there were no such thing as gravity. And any moment the bell would ring. And the doors would open. And Kyle would have to figure out what to do next.

Ding!

Chapter 22

Too fast.

Way too fast.

Kyle hadn't had time to think. Or even catch his breath. Plus, the elevator doors didn't open onto an empty hallway, but smack dab into the middle of a reception area. With an Oriental carpet covering the floor. The kind you'd see in a Gypsy tent. If the Gypsy tent was the size of the Taj Mahal.

On the far wall hung a photograph. A huge photograph. Black and white. Of a charging elephant. Which shook Kyle up. You bet it shook him up. Until he caught his breath. And realized it was only a photograph. And anyway, there was a receptionist's desk between him and those tusks.

Did I say desk?

It looked more like a banquet table. I mean, there were no drawers. Nothing underneath. Just legs and a top. Cool legs, sure. Not chrome. Black. Or flat black. Or matte black. Or whatever you call that cool kind of black that didn't shine and never would, not even if you turned a klieg light on it. The top was glass. Of course it was glass. With the sides buffed so you could see right through it. Like it wasn't even there. Except it was. You could tell. Because sitting on the glass was this space-age telephone and a slick, sleek computer screen as thin as a supermodel's smile.

And that was it.

No manuscripts. No pens. No pads. No paper clip holder. No clock. No Rolodex. No nameplate. No elbows belonging to the receptionist. No receptionist.

Yeah, I know.

The receptionist wouldn't be *on* the desk. He or she would be in the chair *behind* the desk. Which was also see-through, by the way. That's right. Made out of Plexiglas. Kyle could tell because he saw right through it. Because it was empty. As in no receptionist. That's right. Not on the desk. Or in the chair behind the desk. He or she was gone.

Which was all Kyle needed to know.

Because he didn't push his luck. He didn't wait for the receptionist to return. He dumped the pizza into the matte-black trash can next to the reception desk and turned right.

Why right?

No reason. I mean, he wasn't looking for Mercedes Henderson's office. Not then. Not yet. He was looking for a restroom. That's right. A restroom. Because editors had to go to the bathroom too, didn't they? So there had to be a restroom somewhere on the floor. Which either locked from the inside or had a stall. In other words, he was looking for a hiding place.

Because now, without the pizza box, Kyle may as well have been wearing moose antlers, he looked so out of place. I mean, the Boykin Books Building was definitely a non-kid-friendly environment. I mean, kids probably made the scene every year or so, but only as a prop. You know, like a month-old baby to be cooed over or a daughter who just pitched a shutout or a son who finished runner-up in the state tuba contest. Never some kid with a backpack cutting in and out of this cubicle maze all by himself. Because, yeah, it was after six o'clock. But the place was still filled with people. Adult people. Like, a zillion of them. Reading manuscripts. Scrolling their computer screens. Talking into headsets as if they were about to parachute out of an airplane. In other words, they were serious. Really serious. And really busy. Too busy to pay attention to Kyle.

Or so he thought.

"Can I help you?"

Her name was Maureen Turkle. Which, of course, Kyle didn't know. Would never know. The same way he'd never know she'd graduated less than six months before from Bryn Mawr and had a botanist boyfriend living in Argentina who e-mailed her every day, twice a day, and would one day create a vaccine for the West Nile virus (which, of course, Maureen Turkle didn't know either).

All Kyle knew was that she was someone with great big bunches of blond hair who probably worked for Boykin Books and could probably get Kyle kicked out of the building before he made it to Mercedes Henderson's office if he didn't come up with some kind of answer in the next half second. Which meant Kyle wasn't really noticing her blond hair. He was too busy staring at her eyes. Which were staring straight back. And the longer they stared the more Kyle could almost hear those pale green pupils asking, "You lost or something, kid? Or are you trying to get a book published?"

Ha-ha!

It was a joke.

Her eyes were telling a joke. Because she was certain Kyle couldn't be anything more than what he appeared to be—some kid trying to find his mom or his dad or the bathroom or an elevator. Never a secret agent on a mission to sneak into her boss's office and drop off a manuscript.

Which was good.

No, it was perfect.

If the woman with green eyes wanted Kyle to act like a kid, he'd act like a kid. So he winced. And squeezed his legs together. And winced all over again. He didn't hop up and down. He didn't go that far. But by the time he balled his fists and pressed his forearms across his stomach, the woman with green eyes got the picture.

"Follow me," she said.

These weren't the words Kyle wanted to hear. He wanted her to point. Or say, "Over there." Or something that would mean she'd let him go on his own. He didn't want an escort. He didn't want someone waiting outside the restroom. He wanted to slip into the stall, slide the lock behind him, catch his breath, call Lucinda, find out if Mercedes Henderson had already left the building, sneak into her office, drop off the manuscript, and beat it out of there before the guard in the lobby remembered there was a pizza delivery boy who'd taken the elevator up but hadn't taken it back down.

"Who are you visiting?" the woman with green eyes said.

Whoa!

The worst.

I mean, Kyle should have expected this. He did expect it. But that didn't mean he had a good answer. Or any answer, for that matter. So he said nothing. And, instead, scrunched his face into a look of excruciating pain that was meant to tell the woman with green eyes he dared not speak because at that very moment it was taking every bit of his concentration not to wet his pants. Which, of course, was a kid thing. A five-year-old-kid thing, sure, but either the woman with green eyes didn't know much about kids or wasn't that interested in the question in the first place. Because she didn't push it. She simply smiled knowingly and said:

"Well, you won't have to hold it much longer."

And nodded.

To the left.

At the door marked MEN.

And Kyle still said nothing. Not even "Thanks." But instead, scrambled. Or waddled. Or whatever you call it when you keep your thighs pressed together and move your feet forward. Kyle knew he looked stupid. But he didn't care. It was all part of the show. A show, by the way, Kyle happened to be proud of. Since he hadn't opened his mouth. Which meant he hadn't given anything away. And maybe the woman with green eyes would leave him alone now. Maybe she wouldn't be waiting for him when he came back out.

The door swung open. There was no lock. The restroom wasn't made for one person at a time. However, there were stalls. Three stalls. Kyle took the far one. The one next to the wall. And reached for his cell phone. But before he could pull it out of his pocket it began to vibrate.

"Lucinda?" he whispered into the mouthpiece.

"Kyle?" his mom said. "Kyle? Is that you?"

"It's me, Mom."

"Why are you whispering?"

"I didn't know I was."

"Well, you are. What's wrong?"

"Nothing."

"Well, something's wrong. You sound terrible."

"Thanks."

"Don't be cute. Talk right."

"I am talking right. Maybe it's the connection."

"It's not the connection. And you're not talking right. And if this is supposed to be funny, I'm not laughing. And by the way, young man, where are you? Why aren't you home?"

Hmm.

Some spot, huh? I mean, let's pretend you're Kyle for a moment. What do you say? How do you answer? "I'm sitting on the toilet in the third stall on the fifty-sixth floor of the Boykin Books Building, about to sneak into Mercedes Henderson's office and drop off the manuscript Dad told me never to touch"?

"Is everything okay in there?"

That wasn't Kyle's mother. That was the woman with green eyes sticking her head inside the bathroom door and asking Kyle a question.

"What was that voice?" Kyle's mom shouted into the phone.

"Everything's fine!" Kyle said much louder than he intended.

"What do you mean 'everything's fine'?" shouted his mother. "First you whisper. Then I hear some stranger's voice in the background. Then you nearly rupture my eardrum shouting at the top of your voice."

"Is someone in there with you?" asked the woman with green eyes.

"No!" Kyle said.

"'No'?" his mom repeated. "*No* doesn't answer my question."

"I heard you talking," the woman with green eyes said.

"I always talk when I go to the bathroom," Kyle said.

"You do what?" Kyle's mom said.

"Oh," the woman with green eyes said. "Sorry. I'll see you in a minute."

"You'll see who in a minute?" Kyle's mom said.

Beep!

"Call waiting," Kyle said.

"Don't you dare—" Kyle's mom started.

But that was as far as she got before Kyle cut her off.

"Lucinda?" he said.

"Mercedes Henderson hasn't left," Lucinda said.

"But Mercedes Henderson always leaves at six o'clock!" Kyle said. "*Newsweek* said so!"

"You know magazines," Lucinda said.

"What's that supposed to mean?" Kyle said.

"It means get out of there," Lucinda said.

Beep!

"My mom's on Call Waiting," Kyle said.

"What?" Lucinda said.

"I'll see you in a few minutes," Kyle said.

And he cut her off too. But he didn't punch his mom back in. Not right away. First he took a deep breath. And stared at the blinking light. And pictured himself as one of those dogs who has just broken free of his leash and is being called back by his master so that the dog is now looking back and forth between his master and freedom, all the while knowing (or at least appearing to know) that if he runs away he will have to pay for it later, and, of course, running away anyway.

Which was exactly what Kyle did.

No, he didn't run away.

He turned off his phone.

And took another deep breath. And told himself this was it. By the time he made it home his mother would be so furious she wouldn't let him leave the house for the rest of the summer, so he had to come up with something other than sneaking into Mercedes Henderson's empty office and dropping off his dad's manuscript with the note. You know which note. The one Lucinda had written during recess. The one Kyle asked her to write. The one she hadn't signed:

> *Mercedes,*
> *Isn't it time we gave the old folks a love story?*
> *I believe this W. J. Parker has something here.*
> *I loved it. You will too.*

Like I said, it wasn't signed. It was just a note. On a Post-it. Stuck to the title page of *Love in Autumn* under the name W. J. Parker.

Why?

So Mercedes Henderson would think one of her assistants had already read Kyle's dad's manuscript and was crazy about the story. That was the beauty of it. The no signature part. Because Mercedes Henderson wouldn't know which assistant. Which meant she couldn't ask about the book. She'd have to read it herself. *After* Alexa Blake told her about W. J. Parker. *After* Mrs. Gomez talked to her at Mr. Frederico's. In other words, Mercedes Henderson would be pumped. She'd be primed. She'd be excited about *Love in Autumn* even before she read it.

Wouldn't she?

Wouldn't she?

Yes, Kyle believed she would. Which was what he was doing there. In that building. On that floor. Locked inside that restroom stall. Only Mercedes Henderson hadn't left her office at six o'clock the way she always left her office at six o'clock. Which meant Kyle couldn't drop off the manuscript into her empty office. Which meant Kyle was stuck. Since he couldn't wait around much longer. Since the woman with green eyes was bound to become suspicious if he did.

So, yeah, this would have been an awfully good time for Kyle to start to feel sorry for himself. Or panic. Or just plain give up. I mean, his mom was furious. His plan was shot. The woman with green eyes was standing right outside the restroom. And he doubted he'd be able to get away without answering her questions this time around. Because the questions would come. Because the woman with green eyes wasn't about to leave him alone. And there was no window to sneak out. Or air vent big enough to crawl through. And maybe James Bond never had to walk out of a restroom with his hands in the air to be sent home to his mother, but it sure as heck looked as if secret agent Kyle Parker was about to do that very thing. Which, of course, was embarrassing. All over the place. Which is why Kyle thought of Percy Percerville.

No, not his "It isn't what you *are* that matters; it's what people *think* you are."

Not Percy's saying.

The other thing.

The Cynthia Marlow thing.

What if Kyle made a deal with Mercedes Henderson? What if he walked right into her office and told her he could give her the writing scoop of the year if she'd just publish his dad's book?

So, okay.

So as soon as Kyle thought of it he felt ashamed. Not only because he'd promised himself he'd never sink that low but also because it meant he didn't believe in his dad's book.

Or in himself.

Sure, he'd run into a bit of a snag. Sure, things looked bleak. But that didn't mean he couldn't turn things around. I mean, look where he was. Look how far he'd come. All he needed was one more—

Whoa!

I mean—*Whoa!*

I mean, that pep talk he'd just given himself must have paid off. Because it hit him. Like, *POW!* Like, it almost knocked him over. An idea so wonderful and goofy he almost *did* wet his pants.

The truth.

Yeah, you heard me. And, yeah, it was crazy. Kyle knew it was crazy. Even as he flushed the toilet. And unlocked the stall. And walked across the tiled floor. And pulled open the door. And squared his shoulders. And, without blinking, stared straight into those green eyes.

"I'm Kyle Parker," he said in a voice so calm he nearly checked over his shoulder to see who was doing the talking. "My mother and father don't work here. I snuck past the guard in the lobby. Which I know was wrong. And I'm sorry. But I had to. I had to say good-bye. To Philip Harris. He was my hero."

Did I say "the truth"?

It was more like the lie of the century.

I mean, the guy was barely in his grave. And here

Kyle was saying . . . well, you heard what he said. I can't even bring myself to repeat it. I mean, I'm appalled. Horrified. Except, of course, if you're going to lie, why not lie about a dead man? I mean, it wasn't as if Kyle had called Philip Harris a thief or a coward or a cheapskate. Nothing Kyle had just said would hurt Philip Harris's reputation. As a matter of fact, it would help it.

For instance:

One day the woman with green eyes might have children. And one day she might tell her kids about the young boy who snuck into Boykin Books to pay his last respects to an editor. *An editor!* Just like she wanted to be. And probably was by the time she was telling the story. And her kids would be proud of her. And she would be proud of herself. Even more so than she was right now. Peering down at this fine young man. This lover of books.

"A minute in his office alone," Kyle pleaded. "It would make all the difference. It would be something I'd cherish the rest of my life."

It was a good thing Chad wasn't there. He probably would have stuck his finger down his throat. But Chad wasn't there. And Kyle didn't drop his eyes. Or gag over the words. And, yeah, he was laying it on a bit thick even for the lie of the century. Except these last words weren't a lie at all. I mean, if he could be left alone in Philip Harris's office it might just make all the difference. And he would cherish it. Although not quite the way the woman with green eyes probably envisioned.

"Please," Kyle said.

And blinked.

And sighed.

And blinked a second time.

And hit pay dirt.

Because Philip Harris really *was* Maureen Turkle's hero. Almost from the time she was Kyle's age. Which meant she didn't see it as any kind of a stretch that Philip Harris would also be someone else's hero. Nor that someone would like to spend time alone in Philip Harris's office paying his last respects, since Maureen Turkle had spent quite a bit of time alone in Philip Harris's office the past few days paying her last respects.

"Shh!" She put her finger to her lips. "Follow me."

This time Kyle wasn't upset that the woman with green eyes said, "Follow me." Well, he wasn't, and he was. He wasn't because she believed him. But he was for that very same reason. Which sounds like mumbo jumbo, I know. But think about it.

He was going to do what he set out to do. Or, at least, he was going to get a chance to do what he set out to do.

Why?

Because he lied.

And, remember, Kyle wasn't used to lying. Or trespassing. Especially in a dead man's room. No, don't worry. Kyle didn't believe in ghosts. He wasn't worried Philip Harris's mojo would put a hex on him and his father's book for the next seven generations. It was a matter of respect. Pure and simple. Which Kyle seemed to be lacking at the moment. For Philip Harris *and* for the woman with green eyes. Which made Kyle's gut and heart and throat feel the way they always feel when you don't respect someone who deserves your respect. At the same time, however, he was showing a great deal of respect for his father. At least, that was what he kept telling himself. While he also kept telling himself that life had gotten a lot more complicated the past few days.

"We're here," said the woman with green eyes.

And they were.

The room had no number. I mean, I'm sure it had a number. It just wasn't written on or anywhere near the door. Only the name. PHILIP HARRIS. Printed in black on a clear plastic plaque. Which, surprisingly enough, impressed Kyle more than gold leaf or a neon light flashing EDITOR IN CHIEF.

The woman with green eyes caught her breath. And covered her mouth with her hand. Nothing showy. She wasn't making a big deal of it. But Kyle could tell she was getting ready to cry.

Which, of course, was all he needed. Another

reminder of the stunt he was about to pull. But he had to block it out. He had to focus. He had to tell himself she would never know. Not if he pulled this off. As a matter of fact, Kyle could even have given you a pretty good argument at that very moment why it was important he *didn't* tell the woman with green eyes what he was really up to. Because it would only hurt her. It would only make her feel embarrassed she'd let her guard down in front of Kyle and shown just how emotional she felt. Which Kyle realized was about as backward an argument as you could make. But that didn't make it any less true.

"You have one minute," the woman with green eyes said.

And then she pulled a key out of her skirt pocket.

And slipped it into the lock.

And turned the knob.

And opened the door.

"Not a second more," she said.

Kyle didn't pay attention to the dark wood bookshelves covering three of the four walls. He didn't realize the frieze on the wall was from ancient Rome. Kyle didn't even know what a frieze was. Not that it would have mattered. Since he didn't even glance at it. Or the Mayan gold statue of the square-headed woman. Or the fragment of an Egyptian pot five thousand years old.

Instead Kyle closed the door. Fast. Then he looked at

the desk. No, he stared at the desk. Hard. As hard as he ever stared at anything in his life.

Why?

Because he needed a pen. And a sheet of paper. A whole sheet. With Philip Harris's letterhead. As if everything had been planned. Not by Kyle. By Philip Harris. Who Kyle figured had always planned everything in detail and never left anything to the very last second.

But there was no pen.

Or paper.

The top of the desk was empty. Which meant the drawers. Kyle had to open the drawers. But what if they were locked? Or stuck? Or made some squeaky kind of noise that the woman with green eyes would hear?

But Kyle couldn't think about that. Because, no matter what, Kyle had to try to get those drawers open. He had to risk it. He'd come this far. He'd made it this close. And no, he wasn't counting. But he knew at least seven of his sixty seconds were already gone.

Whish!

The top drawer opened. Easily. No sound. Kyle barely had to pull. And there it was. A pen. One pen. *The* pen. Old. You could tell by the way it was worn that Philip Harris had been using it for the past fifty years. The barrel was thick. The top twisted off. It wasn't a ballpoint. It was one of those fountain pen things with a cartridge that held its own supply of ink.

The second drawer had stamps, paper clips, a stapler, a box of extra staples, and even the broken band of a wristwatch. But no paper. Paper was in the third drawer. Thick paper. Heavy paper. Paper with a watermark. Of an eagle. Kyle made out the wings under Philip Harris's letterhead the moment he held it up to the light.

Twenty-three seconds.

Kyle's hand was in his backpack. He was pulling out the manuscript. No zippers. No Velcro. No sweat. All two hundred and sixty-three pages came out on the very first try. Same as he had rehearsed it. Only he'd rehearsed it for Mercedes Henderson's office. With Lucinda's note already written. So all he had to do was drop it on the desk and leave. But the note was no good. Philip Harris would never have left an unsigned note to Mercedes Henderson in his own office on a Post-it.

No way.

But still . . .

Kyle almost chickened out. He almost left the note where it was and dropped the manuscript in the drawer and hoped for the best. But he couldn't. He wanted to. He wanted to take the easy way out. Or the safe way out. But no go. Not even close. Because he knew. Even before he saw the pen or picked up the paper. That Philip Harris would never, not once—not if you offered him ten best-sellers in a row—have written an unsigned note on a Post-it using a ballpoint pen!

Thirty-eight seconds.

Kyle's hand shook. His eyes went blurry. Adrenaline shot through his body so fast all of his major organs felt as if they'd entered a Mexican jumping bean contest. Except for his brain. Which froze. Totally. Ice age frozen. Woolly mammoth frozen. If you asked Kyle what his name was, he couldn't have told you. If you asked him what he was doing in Philip Harris's office, he would have asked you who Philip Harris was.

For seven seconds.

Seven seconds!

Which was, like, forever when you only had twenty-two. Which was how many seconds Kyle had left *before* his brain froze. *Now* he only had fifteen. Which was, like, nothing. I mean, fifteen. I mean, even Vin Diesel couldn't do what Kyle had to do in fifteen seconds. Unless he took it one step at a time:

Fiiit!

Grab hold of the pen.

Fiiit!

Put the pen on the paper.

Fiiit!

Like a gunslinger reaching for his six-shooter:

Mercedes,
Saved this one for you.
Philip

Short. To the point. Nothing sentimental. No gushy stuff. If Kyle knew one thing about Philip Harris, Kyle knew Philip Harris wasn't sappy.

Fiiit!

Pull the Post-it off the title page.

Fiiit!

Place the note on top of the manuscript.

Fiiit!

Hide the manuscript in the bottom drawer.

Fiiit!

Screw the top back on the pen.

Fiiit!

Put the pen back in the top drawer.

Fiiit!

Swipe a sheet of Philip Harris's thick letterhead paper with the watermark of an eagle.

Fiiit!

Slip the paper into your backpack.

Fiiit!

Slip the backpack back onto your shoulders.

Fiiit!

Make sure all the drawers are closed.

Fiiit!

Don't forget to thank the woman with green eyes.

Chapter 23

Why did Kyle swipe Philip Harris's letterhead?

So he could write a letter. Well, actually, so Lucinda could write a letter. And then, of course, print it on the letterhead. Which was easy. No sweat. Kyle told Lucinda what he wanted on the subway ride home. Lucinda wrote it over and over and over until she got the wording just right. And by lunchtime the following day the secret agents were ready for their last mission.

Not that this one had been planned.

No way.

But, as you already know, Mercedes Henderson hadn't left her office the night before at six o'clock. Which meant Kyle hadn't been able to sneak *Love in Autumn* onto her desk. Which meant he had to hide the manuscript in Philip Harris's desk drawer. Which meant the secret agents had to come up with a way to get Mercedes Henderson to look into Philip Harris's desk drawer. And, yeah, Kyle knew the Boykin Books folks would eventually clean out Philip Harris's office, and *Love in Autumn* would be discovered. But that might take weeks. Or months. And Kyle wanted to make sure the name W. J. Parker was still fresh in Mercedes Henderson's mind when she saw his dad's manuscript.

Plus, Kyle had another reason.

No, he wasn't grounded. When he'd arrived home that night, his mother hadn't sent him to his room or threatened him with military school. Though, in a way, he wished she had. Because she'd come up with something worse. Far worse.

She stopped talking to him.

Not the parent stuff.

She still said, "Turn out the light" and "Time to get up" and "Eat your cereal." But that was it. No more, "Gee, that shirt sure looks good on you!" or "Did someone forget to kiss his mother good night?" or "What beautiful blue eyes you have!" You know, the kind of stuff every kid hates until he doesn't get it anymore, and then he feels like there's a hole in his life the size of the Grand Canyon.

Kyle had to do something. And fast. So it was lucky that the next day was a teachers' workday. Which meant no school. Which meant Kyle and Lucinda and Ruben and Chad and Tyrone could take the Lexington Avenue subway uptown to Fifty-ninth Street and cut over to the corner of Fifth Avenue and Central Park where the horse-and-buggy carriages hang out. Yeah, I know. That's also the corner of the kids' zoo. But the secret agents didn't stop to watch the penguins waddle or the sea lions leap or the polar bear swim laps three feet in front of them on the other side of the glass. They crossed the street. They passed the Plaza Hotel. And they didn't stop until they were halfway down the block and, like all the other tourists, stared into that gigantic picture window outside the Bistro.

That's right.

The Bistro.

Hottest lunch spot on the Upper East Side.

I don't mean you sat around sweating or anything. I mean, the Bistro was the place where George Clooney and Brad Pitt might run through a scene from their next Steven Soderbergh movie or J. Lo and Britney might kiss the air on the sides of each other's cheeks. Oh, sure, they ate, too. I mean, the food was good. Great even. That's what got everyone to go there in the first place. But the Bistro was more than a lunch spot. It was *the* spot.

Especially on Friday afternoons.

Which was when everyone who was anyone was there. And, of course, one of those anyones was Mercedes Henderson. Who had a standing reservation. Every Friday at one o'clock. At her very own table. Far enough from the door and tourists. But not so far back she couldn't see. Or be seen.

Which Kyle knew.

All of it. When she arrived. Where she sat. What she could see when she sat there. Which was why the secret agents were outside the window at one o'clock sharp ready to hand her the letter. The trouble was, how were they going to get it in her hand?

Walk right in?

Step right up to the table?

Hand it over?

Sure. That made sense. Except this was the Bistro. On a Friday afternoon. Which was kind of like the Oscar night movie star parade minus the red carpet and silly designer dresses. What I mean is, there was security. *Major* security. Starting with two guys with shaved heads and necks the size of Chad's belly standing cross-armed on either side of the eight-foot-high, polished bronze door.

"I'll just tell them my dad's a plastic surgeon," said Chad.

"That ought to do it," said Tyrone.

"You got a better idea, Opera Boy?"

Leave it to Chad. Insulting *and* inspiring at the same time. I mean, Kyle didn't have any idea what to do with that letter. Or at least he didn't until Chad said "Opera Boy." Then it hit Kyle. Even if he made it past the two muscle guys and inside the door, he still wouldn't be able to get near Mercedes Henderson's table. Because that was the rule at the Bistro. Your table was your castle. No one could approach you. Not an autograph seeker. Not a well-wisher. Not unless you wanted him (or her) to.

No exceptions.

Ever.

Never.

Unless . . .

"Tyrone," said Kyle, "I've got to talk to you."

And he did. Or they did. They talked. Just out of range for Lucinda and Ruben and Chad to hear. Which drove Chad nuts, of course. He couldn't stand the idea that something was going on and he wasn't part of it. Which seemed to happen as often to Chad as it didn't happen to Lucinda and Ruben. Which was why Chad couldn't stand it. Which was why Lucinda and Ruben could.

"Secrets!" said Chad. "Maybe I've got a few secrets myself. Maybe from now on I'll keep them to myself."

"Which is pretty much the definition of secrets," said Lucinda.

"Freckle face!" said Chad.

"Which you'll be glad to surgically remove someday," said Lucinda.

"Ha-ha!" said Chad.

"Ooh," said Lucinda. "Why didn't I think of that?"

Ruben said nothing. Ruben watched and listened. Not only to Chad and Lucinda but also to Kyle, who, it seemed, had just sent Tyrone off somewhere and was walking back to the group. Because Ruben was Ruben. Always watching. Always learning. And, on the basketball court, always trying to outthink the defense. And the more he hung around Kyle the more Ruben saw Kyle was always doing the same thing. Only Kyle was doing it in real life.

"Where's Tyrone going?" said Chad.

"Nowhere," said Kyle. "He'll be back."

"But when he does, ignore him," said Ruben.

"Huh?" said Chad.

"Pretend you don't see him," said Ruben.

"Why?" said Chad.

"Because we're the decoys," said Ruben.

He said it calm. He said it cool. He said it the way you'd figure a guy like Ruben would say it. Not bragging. Not playing the big man because he'd figured it out. Plus he looked straight at Kyle. Who looked straight back. But here's the thing: It wasn't a challenge. What Kyle saw in Ruben's eyes was respect.

That's right.

As if Ruben were saying:

"You're the boss, Parker. Right here. Right now. That doesn't mean I'm backing off on Lucinda. I like her. You know I like her. Even though you like her too. Nah. Don't give me any of that girl-next-door stuff. I know you like her. But it's cool. We'll deal with it. Later. Because that's got nothing to do with this. I'm with you on this. All the way. So tell me what to do, and I'll do it."

"Okay," said Kyle.

"Okay, what?" said Chad.

"We're the decoys," said Kyle.

"Ruben already said that," said Chad.

"Let him talk," said Ruben.

"I think I'm going to like this," said Lucinda.

And so it began:

The last one. The big one. The make-it-or-break-it one. Like in *Mission: Impossible* when Tom Cruise gets the self-destructing message at the beginning of the movie that tells him he has to do what no human being could possibly ever do and never mind asking for any help because we've never heard of you. And, no, none of the secret agents would be hanging in midair trying to crack a computer code or jumping off his (or her) motorcycle and smashing into the bad guy. But, still, they had to walk up to the front door. They had to face down the muscle guys.

Think about it:

The Bistro.

Packed with famous people.

And what do kids like to do?

See famous people. Gawk at famous people. Get autographs from famous people. So all Kyle and Lucinda and Ruben and Chad had to do was act like regular kids. Or *pushy* kids. Maybe even *obnoxious* kids. Which means I probably don't have to tell you which secret agent led the charge.

"Reservation?" cried Chad. "What do you mean I need a reservation?"

"Please let us in!" said Lucinda.

"Just for a minute!" said Ruben.

"We won't bother anyone!" said Kyle.

"I will!" shouted Chad. "I'll bother someone plenty if I don't get through that door!"

General Custer against Sitting Bull. Davy Crockett against Santa Ana. Those were the odds stacked against those two poor muscle guys. I mean, they never stood a chance. Oh, sure, they *thought* they won. They *thought* they were keeping those pushy, obnoxious kids out on the sidewalk. But, as Ruben had said and Kyle had planned, the secret agents minus Tyrone were the decoys. They weren't supposed to get inside. Not even close. They had one job and one job only. Cause a ruckus. Not a bad ruckus. No one was supposed to go to jail. All they had to do was keep things stirred up long enough for Tyrone to make his move.

Did he?

You bet.

Big-time.

Like Kyle said, Tyrone hadn't really gone anywhere. Maybe he walked across the street and petted a horse. Or maybe he ran into the park and actually stood on some real grass. Whatever, he timed his walk perfectly. Arriving back at the scene just as the muscle guy on the right side of the door stepped up to get in Chad's face. Which was all the space Tyrone needed to slip in behind.

Not on tiptoe. Nothing sneaky. Chad had the guy so blind with fury, Tyrone could have tap-danced inside. Tyrone didn't. He simply walked. And pushed open the door. And kept on walking.

Just like that.

Like there was nothing to it.

Except for his heart.

Which was pounding like crazy.

Because making it through the bronze front door was only the beginning. I mean, no way could Tyrone just glide on over to Mercedes Henderson and say hi. The maître d' and waiters would be all over him before he got within five feet of the table. So, no, Tyrone didn't check out the tiled floor or the balcony overlooking the downstairs tables or even the refrigerated display cases stacked with éclairs and napoleons and the most fabulous chocolate chip cookies in New York City. Nor did he notice that he practically stepped on the mayor's foot or impaled himself on the spiked orange hair of In Your Face's female drummer as he weaved his way through those famous or nearly famous people sprinkled among the two-hundred-plus patrons nibbling their *duck à l'orange* and escargots.

Nope.

He sang.

You heard me.

No hesitation. No second-guessing. No last-minute

butterflies that the first note might come out flat. He sang, even though the song wasn't opera. Even though it wasn't close to opera. But a song made popular by, of all things, a cricket:

"When . . ."

No, he didn't *sound* like a cricket. He sounded like himself. Tyrone belted out "When You Wish upon a Star" in a voice so full and rich you'd think he was standing center stage in Carnegie Hall. You see, as shy as Tyrone was in real life, that was as outgoing as he was when he sang. Never mind the noise or the gasps or that no one in that restaurant was the least bit interested in listening to some skinny kid sing.

Tyrone sang.

He walked to the center of the room.

He closed his eyes.

He clenched his fist across his chest.

And he sang that beautiful and haunting tune. Not as if it were being felt by some faraway character in some make-believe song, but as if he himself were experiencing the longing and hopefulness with every word that exploded from his mouth. By the second verse, everyone—and I mean everyone—shut up. Like, totally. Like there was nothing before or after that moment. That song. That kid who moved with the grace of a trapeze artist and hit every note with the force of a broken heart. Who cared that everyone already knew all the words? It wasn't the words that caused the tears to streak down the mayor's face. It was the absolute faith in the kid's eyes when he finally opened them. It was the way those eyes held you.

Haunted you.

Made your heart tell your soul you'd never forget.

And that was before the crescendo. Before Tyrone fell down on one knee in front of Mercedes Henderson. And took her hand in his hands. And clutched it. Caressed it. Holding his gaze with hers as the stomping feet and thunderous roars rattled the silverware and caused the water glasses to shimmy across the tabletops and shatter onto the floor.

And then it was over.

Like that.

Like a snap of the fingers.

Even before the whooping and hollering had begun to fade. Because Tyrone didn't sing for applause. He sang to sing. And anyway, hanging around for a curtain call wasn't part of the plan. Tyrone simply let go of Mercedes Henderson's hand, stood up, and nodded. Once. And that was it. He was gone. Weaving his way back around the tables and half circling the maître d's stand on his way out the door. I don't mean he beat it out to the sidewalk to hang with Kyle and Lucinda and Ruben and Chad. I mean gone. They were all gone. Vanished. Disappeared. As if they never even had been there at all.

Except they were.

They had.

The buzz inside the Bistro said they had:

"Who's that singer?"

"Where did he go?"

"This beats Blue Man Group!"

Mercedes Henderson? How was she doing?

Shocked.

Not *in* shock. But close enough, as far as she was concerned. I mean, the feeling in her hands where Tyrone had touched her had begun to return. Which almost caused her to go into shock for real. Though it had nothing to do with the tingling in her fingertips. It was the note. The one she was holding. The one Tyrone had slipped into her palm when he first took hold of her hand.

No, not a note.

A letter.

On a folded sheet of paper.

Thick paper.

With the watermark of an eagle whose wings Mercedes Henderson could clearly see the moment she held it up to the light.

Chapter 24

A week went by.

Seven days.

One hundred sixty-eight hours.

Ten thousand, eighty minutes.

Six hundred four thousand, eight hundred seconds.

Not that Kyle was counting. I mean, what did he care? His life was swell. Perfect. His mom still wasn't talking to him. Chad wouldn't stop bombarding him with: "So what's going on? Huh, Mr. Secret Agent? How come we haven't heard from Boykin Books? What ever happened to 'It isn't who you are. It's what people think you are'?" Which, no doubt, Kyle could have put up with. Especially since Lucinda and Ruben and Tyrone seemed pretty cool with the idea that it might take a while for a publishing company to come across with a book contract. I mean, Kyle might even have stayed pretty cool himself.

If it hadn't been for his dad.

Who gave up.

Quit.

Stopped writing.

Cold turkey.

Not that Mr. Parker put his foot through his PC screen or burned all his pens in a ceremonial fire. No, it was worse than that. Or more pathetic. At least, to Kyle. As he arrived at the Open Book that following Friday afternoon. As usual, the place was empty. Not of books. Of people. Except for Mr. Jacobson and Kyle's dad. But something unusual did happen. To Kyle. Because Kyle's dad barely turned around. Or even said hi. Because Kyle's dad was too busy nailing a nail into the wall behind the cash register then hanging up the old-man framed photograph of Ernest Hemingway with a fifteen-dollar price tag stuck to the glass.

"Why fifteen dollars?" said Mr. Jacobson.

"Because that's what I paid for it," said Kyle's dad.

"But the pocket in the back!" said Kyle. "The letter he wrote that used to be inside!"

"A pipe dream," said Kyle's dad. "Like all my pipe dreams. Nope. Forget it, son. I'm a washout. A fake. A pretender to the throne. Let some real writer buy it. Let some real writer see if it will bring him luck."

"Because you're not a real writer?" said Mr. Jacobson.

"I've got a hundred and twenty-one rejection letters in my one-room apartment with no tub and no shower to prove I'm not," said Kyle's dad.

"That proves it then," said Mr. Jacobson.

"It proves I won't be getting any more rejections," said Kyle's dad. "Because you can't get rejected what you don't submit."

"Explain that one to me," said Mr. Jacobson. "No, better yet. Explain it to your son."

So there it was. The first day of Kyle's summer vacation. With the dust and old-book smell hanging in the air. Why, Kyle wondered, was it sunny outside? Why wasn't it raining? Or why wasn't the sun sinking in the west? Because that was how his heart felt. Like something was dying. Like everything he'd been hoping for the past three weeks had suddenly come to an end.

Buzz!

Kyle didn't turn around. He didn't want to see whoever the bookworm was that would be slinking into a dusty, old bookstore on a Friday afternoon. Part of Kyle was even beginning to believe that maybe all this was for the better. That maybe his dad's dream was just what his dad said it was. A pipe dream. I mean, come on. So you publish a book? So what? So fifty years from now it ends up gathering dust in a place like this.

Yeah, yeah.

I know.

Who was Kyle kidding?

I mean, first off, he knew deep in his heart this place wasn't so bad. He knew plenty of people were dying to read these books. And, second off, even if the place was so bad it still wouldn't matter. Because that was the thing with dreams. Even pipe dreams. At any moment any dream could turn to dust. That was why they were called dreams.

"I don't believe I'd be selling that photograph for fifteen dollars."

The words drifted over Kyle's shoulder and tickled his eardrum. I mean, I guess. I mean, something caused him to shiver. Not that he'd ever heard that voice before. Though it didn't stop every one of his senses from switching to red alert. Because he knew who the voice belonged to. He didn't know how he knew. There was just something about the playfulness in her tone. Not know-it-all. Not exactly. More like Lucinda when she was getting ready to show off.

Only older.

With even more self-confidence.

"Ernest Hemingway had three sons," the voice went on. "John by Hadley. Patrick and Gregory by Pauline. Right after Hemingway received the Pulitzer Prize for *The Old Man and the Sea,* he had three copies of that photograph made. He didn't sign them. He thought that was too impersonal. Instead he wrote three separate notes to his boys and slipped the notes into the pockets he had specially made on the backings of the frames. But Hemingway was frugal. Some might say cheap. He didn't go to a top-notch framer. One who might have used glue that actually stuck. Rumor has it that all three notes slipped through their pockets and lodged themselves at the bottoms of the frames between the inside and outside backing. Two of the notes have been found. That's because one stayed with the family, and the other was bought by a German collector who took apart the frame. And then there was the third. The one sent to John. Who had a falling-out with his father and was said to have thrown his copy into the garbage along with some leftover ravioli and a fishing rod the great man had given his oldest son on his sixteenth birthday. For years the photograph was thought to have been lost. I say 'for years' since up until two minutes ago, when I was buzzed into your store, no one who knew of the photograph's legacy had any idea it even still existed."

By now, of course, Kyle had long since turned around. And stared. Bug-eyed. As Mercedes Henderson dazzled the three of them with her story. Not only with the words. But also with the way she told it. Which was show-off, sure. But nothing overt. No cocking her perfectly tweezed eyebrows or stretching her streamlined neck. She just talked. And when she finished talking, she walked behind the cash register. And took the photograph off the wall. And satisfied herself that the frame did, indeed, have a pocket attached to the backing. And hung the photograph back up. All the while—or at least, most of the while—keeping those gray-green eyes of hers locked on Kyle's father's eyes.

"Let me introduce myself," she said. "My name is Mercedes Henderson. I'm looking for W. J. Parker. I'm looking for the author of *Love in Autumn*."

Silence.

Nothing.

Zero.

I'm not saying that Kyle's dad and Mr. Jacobson and Kyle shut up. I'm saying the taxi drivers on the street stopped honking their horns, and the people on the sidewalk stopped scuffling their feet, and the birds in the trees stopped chirping, and the wind from the northwest stopped whistling, and the planes overhead stopped flying, and the earth on its axis stopped rotating, and the planets in the solar system stopped revolving around the sun. I'm saying everything everywhere froze. Not forever. It just seemed like forever. Because that was how long it took for Kyle's dad to open his mouth.

"I'm the author of *Love in Autumn,*" he said. "But my name isn't W. J."

"Excuse me?"

"My last name's Parker. But I don't go by my initials."

"But you did receive a letter from Philip Harris."

"A letter?"

"A letter," repeated Mercedes Henderson. "Written to W. J. Parker at this address, then folded up and handed to me by Jiminy Cricket as he serenaded the Bistro last Friday afternoon. This letter. The letter I hold in my hand. The letter that states that Philip Harris, my boss before he died, was so impressed with *Love in Autumn* that he wanted the guy who wrote it to meet Harry R. Boykin, the publisher and owner of Boykin Books, for lunch as soon as Mr. Boykin returned from Palma, Spain. Why? Because Philip Harris, even though he was editor in chief of the third-largest publishing company in the world, wasn't authorized to offer the spectacular amount of money he was prepared to offer an unknown writer for a first novel. That letter, Mr. Parker. Sound familiar?"

Kyle's father didn't gasp. The fluid inside his semicircular canals didn't suddenly slosh around so badly the Open Book and everything inside it spun out of control. He blinked. Of course he blinked. And his left biceps contracted and expanded so fast his whole arm from the socket on down turned into the shortest modern dance movement on record. But, hey. Think of what he'd just heard. And think of where it came from.

Like, nowhere.

Like, out of the sky.

The letter Mercedes Henderson was referring to was, of course, the one written by Lucinda. But Kyle's dad didn't know that. He didn't know where the letter came from. He didn't even know there was such a thing as a letter. How could he? Since he had no idea Kyle and Lucinda had ever seen *Love in Autumn*. Since he had no idea his one and only son would ever have gone back on his word.

"Jiminy Cricket?" Kyle's dad finally managed to mumble.

"Don't be coy, Mr. Parker," Mercedes Henderson said. "You know and I know his name is Tyrone Brown. I know because I asked every music teacher in every high school in New York City. You know because you folded up the letter and stuck it in Tyrone Brown's palm, then sent him off to sing 'When You Wish upon a Star' at the Bistro last Friday afternoon."

Another blink.

Only this blink wasn't panic. Or confusion. Not that Kyle's father had connected all the dots. Not even close. For instance, he didn't have a clue where "When You Wish upon a Star" fit in to any of this. No matter. His eyes lost that deer-in-the-headlights glaze the moment Mercedes Henderson mentioned the name Tyrone Brown.

"Have you met my son?" Kyle's dad said.

"Your son?" Mercedes Henderson said.

"My son," Kyle's dad repeated. "Kyle Parker. One of Tyrone Brown's closest friends."

So that was that. He was trapped. Kyle, I mean. He could run away. But what was the point? What was he going to do? Join the circus? Hitchhike to Alaska and trawl for salmon? Not hardly. I mean, please. I mean, get real. I mean, so he broke a promise. So his dad caught him and would never trust him again.

Kyle Parker:

Liar.

Cheat.

Thief.

He could see it now:

His dad and Mercedes Henderson grilling him on the hot seat until he ratted out his fellow secret agents plus Mrs. Gomez. Maybe Mrs. Gomez would be banned from cleaning another house, and Ruben would be banned from swishing another jump shot, and Chad would never be able to tuck anybody's tummy, and Tyrone would never be able to sing another song, and Lucinda would never be able to read or write or skip down her steps pretending to ignore Kyle ever again.

Funny.

With all of Kyle's planning he never planned on his dad discovering that he (Kyle) was a liar *before* discovering *Love in Autumn* was getting published. Not that Kyle had thought about it a lot. But when he did, he always figured the two things would happen at the exact same time, so his dad's anger and disappointment would be overwhelmed by his excitement and pride. In himself for getting published. In his son for *getting* him published.

One thing for sure, though. There was nothing Kyle's dad could do or say that could make Kyle feel any worse than he felt right now for letting his dad down. In front of Mr. Jacobson. *And* Mercedes Henderson. As if his dad didn't have enough to worry about. I mean, if this were a football game the referee would long ago have blown the whistle and given Kyle a fifteen-yard penalty for piling on.

But this wasn't football.

This was real life.

Which meant Kyle had to face his father. And see the hurt in his eyes. And wait for his dad to explain to Mercedes Henderson how it wasn't him—W. J. Parker or Walter Parker or whatever Mercedes Henderson wanted to call him—who was the mastermind behind these schoolboy pranks. But his son. Kyle Parker. The juvenile delinquent. And Kyle's dad would have. Was just about to, in fact. Kyle even saw his dad's lips start to part. Except they stopped. They froze. Because they were just too darned slow for Mr. Jacobson.

"Mercedes Henderson, I'd like you to meet Kyle Parker," Mr. Jacobson said.

A flash of recognition sparked in Mercedes Henderson's eyes.

"Ah," she said. "Of course. One of the boys from the sidewalk outside the Bistro last Friday."

"I'm sure he is," Mr. Jacobson said. "The same way

I'm sure you wouldn't be here unless you wanted to discuss business."

Well, you can imagine the craziness going on inside Kyle's dad's body. It was like all of his organs decided to switch jobs. His belly was beating. His heart was hungry. His lungs felt like they might die of thirst. Something was up. Something big. He could tell. Or Mr. Jacobson would never have butted in and taken over the conversation. Trouble was, Kyle's dad's brain was too busy trying to swallow or smell or suck in air to figure out exactly what that something was. Which, it seems, went double for Mercedes Henderson.

"And *your* name?" she said.

"Douglas Jacobson," Kyle's dad cut in. "He's—"

"W. J. Parker's personal business manager," Mr. Jacobson cut right back in. "And by the way, Ms. Henderson, thank you for the tip on the Hemingway photograph. But now I think it's time you dropped the tough-guy act and opened your briefcase, so we can all get down to doing what you came here to do."

"Which is?" Mercedes Henderson said.

"Who's being coy now?" Mr. Jacobson said. "Or shall I open your briefcase myself and take a look at what's inside?"

"Huh?" Kyle's dad said.

Mercedes Henderson said nothing. Mercedes Henderson bowed. At Mr. Jacobson. In defeat, sure. But gracious defeat. As she unsnapped her briefcase and pulled out a fourteen-page legal document with the words LOVE IN AUTUMN BOOK CONTRACT printed in block capitals across the top page. Which was as much as Mr. Jacobson read before he put his hands up to stop Mercedes Henderson from handing it to Kyle's dad.

"I believe W. J. Parker's agent deserves to see that first," he said.

"My agent?" Kyle's dad said.

"Your agent," Mr. Jacobson repeated, winking at Kyle. "Your *secret* agent."

Chapter 25

When you're a kid, most of the cool stuff you do is for yourself. Yeah, I know. If you hit a home run your *team* wins, or if you out-debate your opponent your *school* wins. But mostly it's you. You do it. You get the credit. You're the hero. But what kids hardly ever get to do is something for somebody else.

Take Kyle:

He'd been hearing "it's better to give than receive" at least once a week every week since his parents stopped tickling him in the tummy and yabbering "itchy-kitchy-coo!" But he just figured it was something parents said. You know, to make themselves feel better. *It's better to give than receive?* What about the bike you got for your birthday? Or the baseball glove? Or the portable plasma TV? I mean, come on! Who's kidding who here?

Not Kyle.

Not even close.

Not until the night of the book-signing celebration.

Don't worry. I'm not going to get corny or anything. It wasn't as if Kyle *tried* to be a do-gooder. It just turned out that way. Almost as a by-product. But that didn't make him feel any less wonderful that Thursday night the second week of March when he walked into the Open Book and saw those gobs of people squished together drinking champagne and shaking his father's hand and patting him on the back and telling him he'd written the best book they'd read in years.

"Brilliant."

"I cried my eyes out."

"I carry it with me everywhere I go."

So, yeah, *Love in Autumn* was every bit the smash Mercedes Henderson had predicted it would be a month before on *The Tonight Show*. Number one on all the best-seller lists. Rave reviews. Cover stories. Movie offers. Anything and everything Kyle could ever have hoped for except . . .

Except the big one.

You know what I'm talking about.

Kyle's dad and mom.

Were they back together?

No.

Sorry. I guess I could lie. I guess I could make up a they-all-lived-happily-ever-after ending. But that just wasn't the way it went. Don't get me wrong. The Parker family was a lot more happy than it had been the night Kyle's mom told Kyle's dad she'd had it. Kyle's mom and dad just weren't happy together anymore.

Which was a big deal. Don't think for a moment I'm saying it wasn't. And who knows? Maybe someday they might get back together. Especially since Kyle's mom and dad have been going out to dinner once a week every week for the past sixteen weeks in a row, talking about all kinds of stuff—not just Kyle—and coming home happy and maybe a little bit sad, but never (not once, not ever) angry or (in Kyle's mom's case) ready to call Kyle's dad by his first name.

The money?

From the book and movie contracts?

Split right down the middle.

Kyle's dad didn't wait for Kyle's mom to ask. No lawyer was ever involved. Kyle's dad simply informed his accountant that anytime a check arrived to send half to Kyle's mom. And, let me tell you, there were lots of checks. For lots of money. Like, tons. Like, enough so Kyle's mom could pay off the mortgage on the brownstone and maybe someday not even have to work. If she didn't want to. Though, of course, she would work. Since she liked working. Though she sure liked knowing she didn't have to.

And then there was the photograph.

Remember the photograph?

Of course you do.

Well, Mercedes Henderson was right. Dead right. Bull's-eye. Touchdown. Grand slam. Hole in one. I mean, we're talking about a photograph. One photograph. And a note. Let's not forget the note. Lodged at the bottom of the frame. In between the inside and outside backing:

> *John,*
> *A sure hand. A steady eye. A true heart.*
> *Love always,*
> *Papa*

One photograph.

Thirteen words.

Eighty-five thousand dollars.

You heard me. That was what some dot.com guy from Silicon Valley, who obviously didn't lose all his money when the bubble burst, paid for Ernest Hemingway's photograph and handwritten note. Which was now in a separate savings account. The eighty-five thousand, I mean. As a down payment for Kyle's college tuition.

So, like I said, things were looking up for the Parker family.

But that wasn't all of it, of course. I mean, we're running out of pages here, and we still don't know what happened with Kyle and Lucinda.

And you know something?

We won't.

Because it was still going on. I mean, Lucinda hadn't dropped her mad crush on Kyle. But there was also

Ruben. Who scored twenty-six points and had nine assists in the state championship game. Which Roosevelt High won in the last five seconds, by the way. And guess who hit the jumper from outside the key? And Ruben wasn't even a senior. Nor was he about to drop his mad crush on Lucinda. So, like I said, the whole Kyle-Lucinda-Ruben thing was still going on. Strong as ever. And it's anybody's guess how it will all work out.

But here's what we do know:

Chad didn't change.

Sad but true.

You know how some kids can't take a hint even when it's not really a hint but someone screaming right in their face? Well, Chad was one of those kids. I mean, Kyle, Lucinda, Ruben, and Tyrone tried. They tricked Chad into coming over to Kyle's brownstone for an afternoon of Dungeons and Dragons only to bombard the future Dr. Simon the moment he walked in the door with every liposuction and nose job threat that had ever come out of his mouth. But no go. Nothing. Chad even liked it. Convinced himself they were jealous. And, of course, he loved being the center of attention.

Tyrone?

Got a singing contract.

No kidding. You see, Sharon Epps happened to be at the Bistro that famous Friday afternoon and, like everybody else lucky enough to hear Tyrone sing, was mesmerized not only by his voice but also by the way his personality took over the room. Only Sharon Epps wasn't simply some starstruck tourist. She ran the Arts in Kindergarten program for the City of New York. And tracked Tyrone down. And signed him up to teach five-year-olds how to love music the way Tyrone loved music, every other Saturday morning the following school year.

Shakespeare?

See for yourself.

Because he was there. Right there. At the book-signing celebration. Sniffing Kyle's feet. Licking Lucinda's cheek. Jerking his back-left leg up and down like the crank shaft of a locomotive every time Percy Percerville bent over and showed him the top of his shiny, bald head. That's right. Percy had thrown his wig away. Or let Shakespeare eat it. Whatever. It was gone. Though the sparkle in Percy's eye certainly wasn't.

"We've been ruminating, dear boy," he said, nodding gravely at Kyle. "Shakespeare and I. We've been putting our heads together. Brainstorming, as it were. And, after facing down our individual and collective demons, we've decided to grab the metaphorical bull by the metaphorical horns. In short, dear boy, this delicate, high-strung dog and I wish to become your campaign co-managers."

"His what?" said Lucinda.

"Shh!" Percy shushed, putting his finger to his lips. "Top secret. Very hush-hush. You see, dear girl, we happen to be standing in the presence of a future class president of Roosevelt High."

"But—" Kyle started.

"'*But*'?" Percy cut him off. "Again with the 'buts'? We're talking windows of opportunity, dear boy. Pulling no punches. Striking while the iron is hot. The rough and tumble world of high school politics demands clichés and mixed metaphors. And who better to provide you with an unending repertoire of stale phrases and stolen images than that nom de plume of all noms de plume? Who better, dear boy, than"—and here Percy looked around dramatically to make sure no one else could hear before bending down and whispering— "*Cynthia Marlow*?"

Did Kyle know nom de plume was French? Did he know it meant the author was disguising his name?

Not a chance.

Did it matter?

Nope.

Because the moment Percy whispered "Cynthia Marlow" it was like a slap. Like Kyle had been sound asleep, and now every single one of his nerve endings was screaming:

"HE KNOWS! EVERYTHING! RIGHT FROM THE START! THAT'S WHY HE TOLD ME, 'IT'S NOT WHAT

YOU ARE THAT MATTERS. IT'S WHAT PEOPLE THINK YOU ARE!' HE DOESN'T BELIEVE THAT! NOT FOR A MOMENT! HE WAS JUST BEING SILLY! WHY? BECAUSE PERCY PERCERVILLE KNOWS *I* KNOW HE'S CYNTHIA MARLOW!"

But here's the thing:

Percy didn't seem mad. Not even close. Amused was more like it. Grateful even. The way he tapped Kyle on the shoulder with his walking stick, then tipped an imaginary hat at Lucinda. Percy was saying good-bye, of course. But not before answering Kyle's question. The one Kyle never got a chance to ask.

"How—" Kyle started.

"How did I find out?" Percy cut him off. "Second sight, dear boy. A reclusive writer doesn't maintain his veil of secrecy without a highly tuned internal antenna. In short, dear boy, next time you meet Shakespeare halfway up my staircase, you may not want to leave a tooth-marked title page to *The Mists of Amore* languishing between the eighth and ninth steps."

And then he was gone.

Lickity-split.

Before Kyle and Lucinda could breathe again, Percy Percerville wrapped himself inside his cape, gave an imperceptible tug to Shakespeare's leash, and disappeared out the Open Book's front door.

So, okay.

So, Kyle would definitely have chased after him.

As would Lucinda.

If, at that very moment, Mr. Jacobson hadn't switched on the microphone:

"Good evening, ladies and gentlemen. Good evening. My name is Douglas Jacobson. And I'd like to thank you all for coming out this evening. A writer gets to experience his first book signing only once. And lucky us. We're here to share that moment. It is my great pleasure to introduce the author of *Any Idiot Can Clean a House,* Mrs. Carmelita Gomez."

I know.

I did it again.

You thought it was Kyle's dad's night. And in a way it was. Though not his own book-signing celebration. That happened six weeks before. Right here at the Open Book. With hundreds of people lined up around the block waiting their turn to get in. Nope. Tonight was Mrs. Gomez's night. And you should have seen the smile she gave Kyle as she approached the front of the store and Mr. Jacobson adjusted the microphone for her. Kyle's dad saw it. You bet he saw it. Because, in another way, it was Kyle's night too. Because this was the second night the secret agents had a client getting a book published. Which meant Kyle and Lucinda and Ruben and Chad and Tyrone weren't just a one-shot deal. They had other offers. Lots of other offers. From writers, sure. But also from editors who wanted to know who the secret agents had just signed up.

But I said it was Kyle's dad's night.

And it was.

Just not the way you think.

You see, Kyle's dad felt a tug at his heart the moment Kyle and Lucinda went bug-eyed. Over Percy Percerville, I mean. For the past forty-five minutes, Kyle's dad had been watching. Waiting. Biding his time. Hoping for an opening just like this.

"He told me," Kyle's dad said.

"Who?" said Kyle.

"What?" said Lucinda.

"Percy Percerville," said Kyle's dad. "He told me who Cynthia Marlow is."

"He *told* you?" said Kyle.

"He didn't want there to be any more lies," said Kyle's dad. "Not between you and me."

"Oh," said Kyle.

"And there won't be," said Kyle's dad. "Will there, Kyle?"

"No, dad," said Kyle.

"Good," said Kyle's dad. "But that's not all Percy told me. He also wanted me to know what kind of a son I have. Which is why he added that you've known about Cynthia Marlow for months and could have turned him in for the ten-thousand-dollar reward anytime. Except you didn't. You and Lucinda kept the whole thing to yourselves. That's right. He guessed you let Lucinda in on the secret. But he doubted you told anyone else. Even though you could have forced him to help you help me."

"Dad—" Kyle started.

"You think I'm upset?" Kyle's dad cut him off. "You think I'd want to get my book published that way? Let me tell you something. I thought I was proud before. I thought I had a kid who was smart and clever and had more guts than anyone I've ever met. But you know something? I'd trade all that for what Percy Percerville told me this evening. The book? The money? They're wonderful. But achieving your goals without sacrificing your principles? Wow!"

That's right.

That's what Kyle's dad said.

"Wow!"

Which is where I think we'll leave it. Even though Mrs. Gomez was up at the microphone about to say she'd never be standing where she was standing without Kyle's help. And even though Lucinda was about to look at Kyle the way she always looked at Kyle (but this time without the sunglasses). I think we'll leave it here. With the word *Wow!* still ringing in Kyle's ears.